A FOREVER UNROOTING OF JADE AND HICKORY

A FOREVER UNROOTING OF JADE AND HICKORY

MIKKI ROULE

TRIGGER WARNING

There are explicit sexual scenes that
may be too graphic for some.

If these types of scenes make you uncomfortable,
then I suggest you do not continue reading this book.

Suicide and abuse are also depicted heavily in this novel.

Please know your triggers.

For Johnny.
Forever my rooted realm.

*To the girls who like to keep
their villains close at night,
placed firmly within the pages
of a book—so they can rip
them to shreds.*

Two stones were cast out into the mortal world,
this is the unearthing of one...

PROLOGUE
UNKNOWN INLAND LAKE IN MICHIGAN 1969

My haunted feet guided me toward the old hickory again. The worn down trail etched in their memory night after night. It didn't matter to me then why it called. Because when the hickory wanted me there, I would be—without question.

For that reason, just as my feet knew their repeated destination every night since the roots first started calling, my now seventeen-year-old heart felt certain that if the trees were to have a muse, it would be me. Whether it was a whisper of shuffled leaves, a bewitching embrace from their outreaching limbs waiting to be climbed, or a distant memory from the smell of their earthy roots beckoning me to come closer. I always would, even if I didn't then know why.

Each type of tree pulled me inward through whispered promises carried in the evening breeze, filling me with completely unapologetic feelings. For all woods spoke to me, that much is true. And they spoke of a time when I had known them better.

Surely some form of subtle inside joke, knowing how easily they could lure me with their expansive limbs that reached to the sky and their deep roots that weaved toward the core of the earth. But that beaten path told the reality, because of *all* the trees that called my name, it was the hickory that had the strongest pull.

In my youth, I would often find myself rooted at the base of that old hickory tree, being just off the path along the woods of our old family estate. But there was something about that hickory that made it stand out among the rest. An urgent tug at my core reached deep within me to make my blood hum with curiosity. With a need to be near it.

Its claw-like roots stretched down the hill, like it might get up and walk right to me. I thought without a doubt that it wanted to. That as much as I was haunting its strong limbs with my presence every night, I knew the true haunting was reversed.

Within its exposed roots were gaping moss covered holes that seemed they could open up and just swallow me whole into a portal to a world unseen. Secretly, I often thought, I would welcome that idea.

It was a tree so tall and out of place. Its limbs stretched to the heavens, but seemed to then bend down like prison bars, caging in what was found below. For me, the branches offered an unseen protection, much like a warm embrace.

I was a prisoner of my own doing, but I welcomed its warden. A safe haven that urged me there at every waking moment. Some unknown calling of invisible music singing my name through the ever-changing breezes of the seasons.

Only the hickory knows your desires; it seemed to speak in my mind. I didn't know then that these subtle urgings to the hickory were part of something deeper. Built from a legacy I had no part in creating, but that had everything to do with me.

At the base of the tree, a large root burst out and sat there like a jagged finger. A perfect sitting nook. While the other side held a root, that almost seemed to wrap around the whole of the tree. In that spot is where I would spend most of my time.

I lay there in a misshapen circle that if I looked too hard, I swear I could see a glimpse of a sparkle of a life once lived. *Because I had lived it.* Or, as strange as it may sound, I could see a tall form in the distance, always watching from the depths of something sea foam hued. *Because he always had his eyes on me.* At other times, I would hear a shimmer of a whisper that seemed just for me. *Because it was.*

What I didn't know then was that, in those depths, I had lived many lives before—in this world and his—because hickory wasn't just some tree with bark my heart ached to trail my fingers along. No, there was a man beneath its roots that tethered my soul to his. Not even a man, but something more. Something ancient.

That old hickory tree is where my story began in this life. And while it started promisingly with love and lust bursting at the seams with the one who remains tied to my destiny through the realms beneath the trees, it ends quite the opposite. And it ends that way in every life he finds me.

1

BROKEN PIECES
DETROIT 1978

My name is Jade—like the plant, *not* the stone. A distinction my mother would commonly correct people on when I was younger, making sure it was a mistake that was never repeated twice. Why she cared so much forever evaded me, but I know it wasn't malicious in manner. Just one of her many quirks regarding my life, like many mothers have. But whether it was a jade plant or a jade stone, Jade is the name I own.

Growing up, we even had a large jade plant that sat in a cozy corner of the kitchen. I felt nothing towards it. Some days when the sun hit it just right, you could see tiny dust particles dancing off of it like moths to a flame. And I guess in those moments, I felt some vague wonder towards it. Some small bit of connection. But it was a connection based on the fact that I too felt dusty, stagnant, and immovable. As if I were put in a moment of time, I didn't quite belong.

And so, I escaped into my mind and into music. Music always granting me access to some feeling or place in time I felt more attached to. The words of Stevie Nicks holding more value than any relationship in my real life could offer, apart from my late mother.

My mind was another story. It would take me places that

couldn't possibly be real. Daydreams, some might argue, but to me they felt as sure as the ground beneath my feet, anchoring like embedded roots deep within my psyche. Feeling more like visions of moments I swear I've lived before.

These visions that played out in my head stopped being a habit—they became who I was. Tugging me toward a life of what some might see as quiet contemplation, when in reality my mind was plagued by a series of movies playing out in real time from *another* time altogether. Scenes so real that I felt a nagging feeling telling me something vital was missing. Or someone.

I was called many names in my younger days; mysterious, spacey, and, always my favorite, devoid of reality. I'd happily claim each adjective as my own. While I hold no validity in people's perception of me, there is always a small smidge of truth buried within it.

In all honesty, I grasped at a love my mind invented—idealized and out of reach. A version of love that I felt like I knew on some base level of my being, but never feeling like I could actually picture in this reality. Even when my feet were planted firmly on the ground, something always tugged me elsewhere, some place deeper—some place that felt more like home than this in-between liminal life.

And even now, as a twenty-six-year-old, I still hold on to that deeply romanticized idea of love. A love that dances you around on a balmy moonlit night in the presence of friends, spinning until you only see each other. One that creates handmade treasures that speak directly to your heart, or even transcends time to search for you no matter the circumstances. I realize I am the odd one out, but that is the love I have been looking for, and I'm starting to think it doesn't exist for me.

Thankfully, I hold that level of adoration for the treasures in my shop. The touch of my hand imbuing it from them, as well as gracing me with a past glimpse of a tall and dark man handing it to a faceless girl about the same age as myself. These vaguely nostalgic items in this shop are the reason I stay.

Working at a vintage art and collectibles gallery has its perks. For one, I get to roam the cities in search of anything old with monetary value to sell in my mother's shop. At least I used to when she was alive and still felt enthusiasm toward the hunt, but her death put a halt to the giddy exploration of hidden treasures.

Getting to learn the history behind those objects is another perk I am fond of, and one that has not yet faded. My mother and I would spend hours researching, and I can still invoke the joy we felt when we cracked the historical code on a turn of the century Art Nuevo piece from France that last spring she was still with me. She passed when I was nineteen, and this store is what she left to me, and all that I have left of her.

Nonetheless, here I am at 8:00 a.m. on a Sunday, pushing the key into the old copper lock, ready to start another morning. A memory of my mother doing the same morning routine fills my thoughts, her face beaming down at me.

I see her expression most mornings when I set the worn key inside its lock, but today the mirage of her face seems off—worried, fearful. Before I can dive deeper into the meaning, I am pulled out of my memory by a mass of crows in the giant oak tree next to our lot, cawing a special good morning.

"Good morning to you, too," I say dryly, looking up toward the nearby tree at the mass of black feathers hidden beneath a sea of deep green leaves. A small breeze rustles through the tree above and caresses my skin. The summer heat feels welcoming. Only three months of this makes one long for a climate that holds this kind of warmth throughout the entire year.

Carya, the stray tabby cat, comes brushing along my feet and sneaks in once I have the door just barely open, almost tripping up my brown suede double strap Mary Jane clad feet. A recent fashion splurge that had a lot to do with the bottomless pina colada drinks my best friend Lollie and I had prior to shopping.

"And hello to you, sweet girl." I scratch her orange striped back, and she arches just enough to show she is happy to see me.

After one wild stormy night, this fluffy bundle of fur turned up at the shop door as a kitten unannounced, starving and in need of a warm place to sleep. Over the past three years, I have watched Carya grow from a kitten to the soft lug I've come to call my own. Her soft meow is accompanied by another warm, devoted brush against my leg. The feeling is mutual, and she knows it.

My little shop of dated eccentricities is tucked between a tiny bougie flower shop and an inconspicuous and proper law office in Detroit. I smile, noticing how the soft smell of fresh blooms wafts around me. I enjoy the way it mixes with the archaic smell of the eclectic findings of my shop, which is why I usually keep my door open to welcome the aroma.

A frame of chipped salmon paint surrounds the stained-glass window that adorns the top of the door. Quiet reminders from the paint job years ago when we first had a more solid and hopeful vision for the place. A time much different from the position I find myself in now.

The ancient items surrounding me take shape in my still-groggy eyes as I walk into Moon Shadow Collectibles. Romantic-era prints line the walls—finds from estate sales, scavenged with my mother in the old homes of Detroit's once-wealthy. Some would say the prints are excessive, morbid even, but I've always had an affinity towards that dark, ethereal era of art. My mother would roll her eyes whenever I'd ask her to look for pieces of this era, but she always did. Now they greet me each morning like a quiet echo of her infinite love, even as her presence fades.

I see her looking at me now with her sage eyes that hold a wisdom I can't even begin to interpret. Eyes are funny that way. They stay locked in my memory of all the words that were never said, but clearly conveyed in one glance. Her eyes communicated a lot of unspoken knowing when she was here, and they stay with me, even when my own close shut at the day's end.

The store comes to life as I move to each switch and scrutinize some of the pieces I've seen every day for the last ten years. The art déco collection of old lock and key sets sparkles in its respective place next to the Romanian pottery vase we found by chance at an estate sale in Hamtramck. I trace the rough grooves of the spiky floral design as though my very own hand had etched them.

The half-melting candles in various candelabras drip with hardened wax as if frozen in time waiting to be released, and a first edition *Frankenstein* book that has a not for sale sticker underneath it all greet me in silent earnest. Every one of these items I've cleaned, dusted, and researched over the past decade. All hold a small claim on my heart.

One piece in particular sits on the counter right next to the cash register. It is a willow tree made completely of jade stone. And while our old jade plant left me with no feelings, the cascading delicate green branches of this stone willow speak to me as if it were embedded in my soul. It sits heavy in the cradle of my palm as I give it careful consideration. A piece I've always loved, and a piece my mother told me never to sell.

My mother would take it with us wherever we were living, and it seemed almost attached to her since before I can even remember. And while I would always try to research it, I could recover no glimpse of its past or what time period it came from.

A small crack lines the inside curve of the trunk, but the faint line only adds to its allure. As a teen, I would look deep within its green sheen searching for the feeling it gave me. Hoping it might be something tangible that I could wrap my hands around. But delicate things don't yield to the kind of wanting I carry.

Brushing my fingers along the base of the willow, I set it back in its place, surprised at myself that I even had the nerve to touch it at all. There is a boisterous caw from one of the crows that collect outside my door just as the phone rings. My feet click against the oak floorboards, while I make my way to the telephone attached to the back wall. Its mustard yellow color, a stark contrast to the dated brown and blush pink pinstripe wallpaper behind it.

The voice that greets me is bubbly and full of way too much pep for this hour of the day. Lollie. She is trying to get me to come out for another round of bar hopping tonight.

As much as I try to be a homebody in the evenings, Lollie's go get 'em attitude always gets me feeling like maybe there is something to look forward to with a night on the town. Perhaps there could be a man to live up to the romantic expectations I've fabricated in my head. More often than not, it ends in poor decisions and a very unappealing headache the next morning.

"You can't pull another 'I have to clean the shop' today." Lollie exclaims into the phone. "I will not let you stay chained to a store that has one to zero customers a day." Her voice is exaggerated as if I'm at the end of my journey with this shop.

"Wow, that's harsh," I say under my breath. I actually quite love this quiet shop, and Lollie knows that. She gets desperate when trying to get me to play along with her shenanigans. I toy with the stretchy spiral phone cord as I replay her words again. I wonder if I will ever not get sucked into her go arounds.

"I know. But there comes a time when you need to listen to your best friend in the *whole* entire universe and have a night of forgetting. You can go back to remembering all your responsibilities tomorrow. *Please* Jade. For me?" I can almost see her pout through the receiving line, and I look up to the ceiling every bit as annoyed with her persistence.

"Ugh, fine," I give in as I roll my eyes out of habit. My worst habits are always brought out with phone calls involving my dear friend, but I wouldn't have it any other way.

"Great, because I also just bought some super groovy dresses that need to be put to use!" Lollie throws in, knowing I love to dress up as much as I love going out.

Her eagerness for me to come out is palpable. It's not her fault, though. There was a time when I couldn't even get out of bed most days. To be honest, I think she keeps me busy so I don't think about losing my mother too much. Other times I think she wants me to forget completely.

The months after losing my mother are ones I would like to forget, too. I've gotten much better. But the windows that haven't been washed in weeks, and the shelves that sparkle with dust from the little light that comes into the shop through those same sad windows, say otherwise.

I put the phone down and shake my head with a lingering smirk on my face. No matter how hard I try to stay in my comfortable hermit mode, Lollie always sways me out. She is my day-one friend after all. And as much as I like to keep to myself, she seems to have wiggled her way into a permanent spot in my heart.

We grew up together during the most formative years of our lives. The years when boys reigned supreme and the Ouija board was a must at every sleepover. We were just coming into our own then. Caught between figuring out who we were and who we might be. Sometimes, I find I'm still in the midst of figuring out both of those things.

Lollie's mom died when she was a baby, and her dad, whom I never actually formally met, spent all his time working. Because of that, Lollie basically lived at my house once we settled down in Detroit. My mom treated her as her own, even though she was the sole reason I ever got in trouble. She has a way of talking me into even the worst situations, and with that being said, tonight I will go be a part of her nightlife world.

If you follow the trail of muddy cat prints that line the floor behind the store register to a small white back door, you will find a tiny room that holds a variety of miscellaneous items. A catch all kind of place, you might say. Within it sits a bunch of cleaning supplies, paperwork, and items for the shop that I have yet to research. I pull out the broom and let the stiff bristles swipe against the hard floor. Bits of dust plume into various cracks and crevices, never to be seen again.

Carya finds the warmest sun-soaked spot on the floor to curl up on, as the morning sun shines through the windows. I place the broom against the wall next to her. As calm as most days are here, I feel antsy. An uneasiness stirs the air and sets me on edge like the scratching of tiny fingernails inside my belly.

Outside, the traffic picks up as the other building owners flick on their open signs. It's always busy in this city, with men in business suits and women trying to make themselves known in a world ruled by those said men. That's why I feel lucky to have this shop. I don't have to fight to prove my worth. This shop and I just are. But I feel a collective stirring when I see women living up to their true potential and fighting for what's theirs in this city that for years has discredited their voice.

My fingers feel for the switch to flip my neon sign to open, and wave to Ashton, who owns a pub across the street. He shoots a friendly wink my way while actively trying to prop his heavy bronze-framed door open. His smile shining through the gleam of the storefront glass.

Ashton set up his shop shortly after my mother and me. He became a friend I never knew I needed. The friend I found in him being so entirely opposite of Lollie. Lollie is loud and wild, with sharp edges she softens with her charm, while Ashton's sweet smile and warm understanding has kept me feeling comfortable and safe for many years.

Not far from the very ordinary cash register sits my most prized possession. My darling record player. *Elenor Rigby* by The Beatles works its way through the speakers. It is a solemn song, but that type is what my soul craves most days.

Once the music starts, the store darkens. An overcast of clouds swims over the golden orb in the sky just as the two crows out my window squeak wildly. I think I hear the echoing call of another bird, which seems out of place, but with the hustle of the streets it quickly gets drowned out. The edgy feeling in my stomach strengthens.

Coffee in hand, I take in the store my mother and I put so much love into, wondering how I let it come to this. Perhaps if I invested more love and care into what's left, it would ease some of the sorrow from losing my mother. Maybe even lighten up my so-called dismal attitude, according to Lollie. But I know it would only cause me to drown more in my memory of her.

The warm, rich coffee hits my lips, breathing in its aroma through my nose, careful to take it all in. This part of the day is always one of quiet where I can gather my thoughts before planning the day. Could this be all I plan for in this life? Shop duties and late-night dives? I had hoped I would have more to call my own at this age, but grief does funny things to one's mind. Sticks a dagger into hopes and dreams, and bleeds them dry of anything that may have come of them.

Carya is now perched by the window, seeming to look out at whatever the weather outside is trying to say in the quiet battle between the sun and the clouds. A blur of bird wings beat past it, causing Carya to startle and let out a mangled meow before scampering away toward the back room.

But before she does, she knocks the broom that I forgot to place back in the closet forward into the jade stone willow tree, which brings it crashing to the floor. The silence after is deafening until I climb out of my shock, and look at the outcome of her nervous excitement. I gasp, coffee sloshing as I leap forward, heart pounding beneath my thin silk top. Panic shoves me toward the scattered remains of the jade willow.

In that moment, I am broken too as I look down at the floor. Then, something else entirely. Oddly awake? More *alive,* even. An odd combination for me, and one I don't quite expect. The quiet slumber of my emotions I am so used to, transforming into a new debut of thrilling sensation. The defeat does come eventually when I realize what has become of my mother's beloved willow.

Near tears, I frown down at the only item my mom held much meaning to. It is not glass, so it doesn't break off in small shards, but into large jagged chunks. Looking closer, there seems to be a hollowed-out part within the base of the stone that didn't fracture.

I bring myself to floor level and pick up the largest hollowed piece. I peek inside, thinking of all the things my mother told me to keep safe this was the most important. And, of course, I not only break it, but quite literally destroy it. Her soft voice wouldn't scold, but I can imagine the disappointment that would fill her earthy stare.

As I peer in, I see something metal that doesn't quite belong. The dull metallic object shimmies out into my palm, recognizing it immediately. A ring. So different from any other ring I have ever seen. Enchantingly beautiful, as if made by a tiny team of fairies. The thought sends goosebumps across my arms. My mother would call them truth bumps, because that's exactly what they spoke of.

The old tarnished golden metal sends an instant shock through my system that tells me this object is extremely old, archaic even. I hold it still to inspect it. The warmth of it spreads on the palm of my hand, making its presence felt on a very cellular level.

Its band is a deep bronze color that forms a bundled circle of leaves. The leaves look so much like those of the long-standing hickory tree I would gaze under in my youth. But instead of being made from bronze, they are inlaid with green stones matching the same jade green of the willow tree that now lay in chunks on the wooden floor of my shop. My mother could not possibly have known this ring lay hidden inside, but I can't help but think of how fiercely she protected it throughout the years. For what other reason would that be but this?

I hold out the ring and linger the circular object above my left ring finger. My hands won't keep still. The ring hums with a quiet gravity, a quiet belonging singing from it to me. A trance of its magical beauty taking over the moment.

I get it to just the tip of my finger, but I am stopped when a whimsical chime reverberates through the walls of the store followed by a breeze of balmy July air causing me to look towards the door. The door always chimes when someone enters, but this time it is followed by a nagging feeling that creeps rhythmically along my skin.

It's not an unwelcome reaction, but one that holds the potential of many possibilities that I'm not ready for. My whole life I've dreamed of this type of feeling. The one you know will change the trajectory of your life, and standing at the door is the reason.

Two very intense eyes the color of the deepest sea green meet my own. Instantly, my mind goes to a tangle of roots. The smell of damp earth clinging to a simple white dress of another era. I think of the old estate we lived at when I was younger, where the hickory called me close, and am lost back to a vision when I knew who I was in my purest form. It is but with a blink and the memory fades, but the man is still there.

2

INHERITANCE
DETROIT 1978

I think I will always replay this first impression, before our words got in the way. The subtleties of the sunlight outside mixed with the darkness held within, creating a flush stillness that doesn't speak of any expectations. Our gaze at each other? Well, that tells a different story completely.

The man who enters my shop strolls towards me in his crisp button-down shirt and black dress slacks. His shoulders pull tightly at the shirt fabric, threatening to make it burst at the seams. *I wish they would.* His deep brown hair looks as if he tried to hold it back with hair gel, but it doesn't want to behave. *That makes two of us.* Pieces are falling just above his brow line. And just under those fallen tresses are two very faint scars etched above each eyebrow; slightly raised as if whatever is lurking below his smooth skin is trying its hardest to stay just below the surface.

His skin is a deep rich color, while intricate branch-like designs line his forearms and weave out from under the sleeves of his rolled-up shirt. I can't tell if they are tattoos or birthmarks, but they look as if born a part of him. If this were the day God struck down Lucifer to be banished amongst the mortals, I'd swear it is who I am looking at now. But maybe that's just wishful thinking, as my perfect idea of love becomes irrevocably blurred with every second my eyes are glued to his. As he walks closer to the counter, I silently applaud myself for finding my words. *See, Jade, you can do hard things.*

"Good morning, can I help you with something?" My voice sounds small and weak, and I wonder if it is even attached to my body at all. Unshed tears still drying on my cheeks over the smashed willow. The devilish man looks down at me where I still sit on the floor cradling the broken bits of it, and he tilts his head curiously.

"Why yes," he dares to smirk before he says, "But, I think you're the one who needs help, Jade." His voice is dangerous, wrapped in a mix of silk and arrogance that lingers far too long against my skin. A perfect introduction that needs to be stopped so I can go back to living in my handcrafted gloomy glass case.

Wait, how does he know my name? I must ask this out loud, because a look of annoyance enters his gaze. I follow the path of his stormy eyes that link to the picture of me hanging on the wall towards the front of the shop, my name marked boldly under it. *Oh, of course.*

"Let me clarify. I am from a small town in Louisiana on the outskirts of New Orleans. Just here to talk some business." I'm silent within his pause, waiting for his next words. "You've come into quite an inheritance. A large estate down there, including everything inside it." An estate? I try to rack my brain for any relatives my mom may have had, but my mind comes up blank. Surely this must be a mistake.

"Inherited? That makes no sense. I'm sorry. Who is it from?" I ask. Skepticism written all over my face as my eyebrows cinch together to create the deepest furrow lines.

"Your uncle." *An uncle?* My mother never mentioned an uncle, or any other family for that matter. The man must sense my confusion and dips his head so that our eyes meet once again. He holds my gaze for a time too long, causing fiery warmth to flood my body. Do I know him? No, definitely not. But there is a familiarity there I can't deny.

"I work as an estate lawyer. I've come all the way to this city to hand-deliver these papers to you on behalf of your uncle's will. And if you don't mind, I would like to be on my way now," he explains, saying the word city with a hint of disgust that is clearly visible on his face.

My old glass shield slides back into place—he's like the rest, after all. But there is something magnetic that keeps me slightly open. Letting his influence find me, hoping to be surprised.

I'm sensing I might actually be in need of a night out after all. Or, quite possibly, the allure of this indifferent man with his attempted combed back hair and ocean deep eyes is actually affecting the girl who swore off thinking of men as anything other than just existing.

Danger, my mind tries to say, but my body says a totally opposite thing. One side of his mouth tips up, as if he were silently reading my thoughts. His mouth opens, and my gaze lingers as his lips part.

"You must be at the house within the next month in order to sign more paperwork." And with that comment, he turns on his heels. "I left my number in the folder in case you need me, as well as a map to the estate. It's nearly impossible to find on others," he adds, sounding unsure if he wanted to relay that last bit of information.

When he reaches for the doorknob, he hesitates, and if I weren't staring at him so closely, I might have missed his expression. A dense emotion sears through him in the shape of a clenched jaw and closed eyes. But then, he straightens his shoulders, opens the door and leaves. Meanwhile, I am left standing with my jaw on the floor along with the destroyed pieces of jade at my feet.

I'm starting to question if the encounter even happened by how fast the man came and went from the shop. Dropping a bomb of massive proportions on everything I knew of life at this moment. Could the Twilight Zone actually be a real phenomenon that I can't seem to snap myself out of?

My body struggles to keep my spine straight with all the emotions freely flowing through my still shaking limbs. Not only was I unsettled about the hidden ring and devastated that I broke my mother's most treasured item, but then to add in an inheritance all within the half hour. This is a day for the books.

I look over the papers that were so nonchalantly placed in my hands. Could I really be the owner of a house, in a place I have never been, that was an uncle's I have never known about? It seems insane, and that is how I feel.

The underlying heat within my core bubbles its way back up to the surface, leaving me wanting to crawl out of my skin. I'm entirely overwhelmed with the array of sentiment brewing within me, and now more in need of a drink than I think I have ever been before. It's no surprise I close the shop early with a clove in my still trembling hand, more than happy to take Lollie up on her offer of a night out.

3
NIGHT OUT
DETROIT 1978

"Two more shots of tequila for my friend," Lollie practically screams at the thin blond bartender. Dreading what two more shots would make the night into, but also knowing that at that moment I would not deny them after the day I just had. A day that included a not so charming, but intensely handsome green-eyed man and a house that is apparently now in my ownership.

After tall, dark and handsome left, I got on the phone right away. Dialing one of the few numbers left in the stack of papers the man put in my hands. I needed to see if I truly had an uncle who left me a house near New Orleans. Much to my disappointment, the call was not answered by the deep baritone I was hoping for, but it wasn't fruitless.

In fact, I discovered I was willed a lot more than just a house. In a small town in southern Louisiana named Racine, sits a fully furnished mansion with a one hundred-forty-acre wooded lot. And even a couple of old cars from varying decades. I tried looking for the town on the map I had on hand in the shop, but it must be too small a town, for there was nothing to mark it. Odd that it's clearly marked on the map the man gave me.

After an hour or more of inquiring about wills and trusts, I decided to head down in the next few days to see the house for myself. *But* for now, as I look at my very darling, very blonde best friend, who must have learned a new smoky eye technique, I am going to enjoy this night out and pretend I haven't a care in the world. And thankfully, the alcohol coursing through my body is doing just the trick.

I feel the wobbly mellow of the last three shots we consumed take effect as I look out at what surrounds me. Of all the bars Lollie could have picked, this one is definitely the least disagreeable. It sits a few doors down from the corner of Sixth and Lafayette Boulevard, and sees its fair share of traveling businessmen come through its doors every night.

The bar's rich mahogany moldings and dark grey walls create a dreary ambiance, especially when mixed with the cigarette smoke. But that quiet sadness also holds a feeling that is inviting and warm in its melancholy magic. I've always been a sucker for that kind of unique charm.

The dance floor is merely a small tiled open area next to the jukebox. And when you look up at the giant disco ball above, it sets a luminous glow much like the full moon on a clear night in this concrete city. It almost seems out of place as it releases a glittery sheen across the bar that bounces off the glassy-eyed patrons occupying the floor below.

I down each shot that Lollie hands my way knowing we must be nearing number three, and she looks at me with eyes full of shock.

"I can't believe your mom never told you about her having a brother." She grabs my hand with a little squeeze to give her words extra effect. It's an unnecessary action, because I've been living with the shock of the situation all day.

"You and me both, Lol. But can we not right now? Let's just enjoy tonight." It's clear to me that my brain has hit overload, even though Lollie seems not to have picked up on that. So I add,

"I am not adult enough to think about all this right now." Or maybe not sober enough is what I mean to say. Lollie looks at me with a sideways glance and the widest grin.

"You're twenty-six..." We both burst out laughing immediately after the words leave her dark pink lips, realizing how ridiculous I sound. In my defense, when you've grown up with someone for so long, you always feel a bit adolescent when you're with them.

To get out of her knowing glare, I try to lure her to dance, nodding my head at her pick of suited men near the dance floor. Dancing is always the best option. And I feel like I *should* be dancing with what Lollie made me slip into for the night.

I'm wearing a metallic pink mini dress with bell sleeves and a plunging neckline that leaves little to the imagination, but I like it. It makes me feel like a big pink moon shining above an endless, deep sea. A sea that matches the eyes of a *very* alluring man I met today.

Frustration is a new embodiment I've taken on today. I am still kicking myself that I didn't get his name, and I would be lying if I didn't say I thought about him more than a couple times after he stormed out the door. I'm trying to wrap my head around the fact that I could even find someone who clearly didn't want to be in my shop so appealing.

I discussed little with Lollie about the man. I know her ways too well. She would want to know all the details, and I don't know that I trust myself not to reveal more of my lust fueled feelings than I want. She'd probably scout him out and bring him to my doorstep if she knew what he sparked beneath my skin.

"OK, now I *know* something is on your mind, but I won't pry anymore," Lollie announces while she reads my face intently, then gives me a quick peck on the cheek.

I smile, grab the shot glass in front of me and down it. Is that number four? Trouble will brew at this bar if Lollie buys any more. She can drink like a fish, while I drink more like a manatee floating to the bottom of a dark void with every shot I put in my body.

I focus on Ashton. He follows us on most of our outings, playing the distant bodyguard in case any of us get any unwanted attention. His good-hearted nature is infectious, so I never mind when he tags along. Most people find his bright glow a beacon for positivity, which is why he's currently surrounded by his own group of friends at the table across the bar with a drink in his large hand.

His positive attitude was nonexistent when he heard of my inheritance. I found him quick to tell me all the ways Louisiana is a terribly unsafe place to live. He is just worried, I know, but the seed of distrust he has of the place took root deeply.

Ashton throws a wink at us from across the room, and Lollie can barely hold her disdain as her eyes flip up to the ceiling and then back to me.

"Why is he always here?" Lollie gripes, annoyed, and for good reason. Lollie and Ashton have a history. The on and off type of history, and right now they are *very* off. I chuckle under my breath as they stare at each other with a look that seems it could open a wound.

Seeming to be in the middle of this standoff, I take the next best course of action. I grab Lollie's hand and pull her toward the dance floor. *Maggie May* is playing on the jukebox. A favorite of both of ours. It's the perfect song to forget to, and that is what I hope to do.

I let the music soothe me into a trance-like state while Lollie dances with her arms above her head, wearing the biggest grin on her face. My feet move of their own accord, stumbling every once in a while. A sure way to tell I've had one too many drinks, but I'm not worried about that now.

We dance for what seems like an hour. The sparkle of the disco ball lands in iridescent orbs on my face. I lift my face so the orbs are all I see, each speck looking like a moonflower I've seen somewhere in my past. The tequila is doing its job of loosening my muscles and my inhibitions. My thick hair falls down, just skimming my shoulders, and I'm aware of a shadow of a palm on the small of my back.

Slightly startled, I spin around to shove whoever it is away. My hands meeting mist from a man's form, smelling of flowers that open under the watch of the stars. And then, no one. My stomach relaxes as I realize it was just another hallucination of a moment that never was.

Recognizing I'm maybe in need of a break. I turn to Lollie, my mouth forming words to let her know I'm going to get some fresh air. She is consumed with the beautiful olive-skinned man next to her. Her arms linked around his neck as they sway to the music.

She moves through flattery as if it's a language she herself invented. I've never learned that way of speaking. It breeds more complications than it's worth. She gives me a quick wink of her eye, and mouths back that she'll be right behind me. I laugh, because she looks anything but.

I stumble across the old, whiskey-stained carpet of the bar toward the main entrance to the street outside. The question of why a bar owner would pick carpet as its flooring of choice flows through my mind. I can always count on these deep, philosophical thoughts when liquor is involved.

I pass Ashton, who is shamelessly staring at Lollie, while pretending to listen to a pretty brunette sitting on his lap. My platform boots do nothing for my balance, and I all but fall out toward the entry. I just barely catch myself on the deep-colored doorframe, my palms thankful for the support. The thick wooden door takes a bit of effort to open, but I finally let the warm midsummer night air envelop me as I make my exit.

There isn't a soul outside, which is odd for a Saturday night. I feel a little uneasy, but reach inside my purse for the one thing I need most when booze swirls through me. My fingers find the small pack of cloves at the bottom, and I instinctively fish one out. Shuffling through my purse again, I exhale in irritation at forgetting my lighter and lean up against the building in a defeat of my own doing.

I close my kohl-rimmed eyes, the unlit clove still hanging lazily between my fingers, and let my thoughts drift a bit, sobering me up.

What the hell am I going to do with a house a thousand miles away from here? I can't possibly wrap my head around what my future now holds. I take a deep breath with my eyes still not wanting to open. The smell of white midnight blossoms and smoky whiskey fills my senses.

"Don't you look wildly out of place here," a smooth voice rattles me out of my head. My eyes open to light acorn brown ones with a remarkable ring of silver around the iris, and messy moonlight blond hair attached to a very well dressed male in a dark blue fitted suit. Well, he *would* be well dressed, but his tie is skewed to the side and the top two buttons of his shirt are undone. There is but one thing a suit in this city usually means: a night at the overpriced hotel and a story that never makes it past the city sign.

He holds out a match, which I realize is meant for me. I quickly light my cigarette and thank him. Not putting it to my lips right away and letting the smoke linger up, as I take a deep inhale through my nostrils. The aromatic smell is what I really buy them for, anyway. The semi clean shaven man glances sideways at me like he is realizing this secret truth.

High above, his hand presses on the wall. His acorn eyes slowly look me up and down, which must have made a crimson blush crawl up my neck and appear on my cheeks. He is looking at me like a rose in bloom needing to be plucked. His pouty bottom lip and thick sharp eyebrows are a strong contrast to his almost white blond hair. It's clear to anyone with eyes that his allure in this moment is undeniable, and I have a feeling he knows it.

He smirks a lopsided grin at me, studying my face to the point I think I may need to turn away. On any other day, I might indulge myself and take this further. He is just my type, and I will not deny how the streetlight hits the angles on his face in just the right way, leaving an almost shimmer along his jawline. He's too pretty for his own good, a problem I'm seeing clear as the cloudless night sky. And that grin—crooked and smug and nothing I can move my eyes away from—hooks me harder than I want to admit, making me wonder how he might use it against my skin.

But today has already been a lot for my mind to sort through. The events have brought my anxiety to its highest peak. I know I won't be taking this anywhere tonight, but I linger longer on his lips for the sake of looking. Three heartbeats pass, and I finally find my boldness to address him.

"Well, if you don't mind, I need to find my friend. Thank you for the light and the very unsettling stare-down." I announce. Being that his arm is still braced against the wall, I have to squeeze in between it and him. He doesn't show any sign of adjusting to let me by.

As I shimmy my way through, I keep my eyes pinned to his, biting my lip on instinct. He flicks his gaze from my eyes to my mouth and then back up. His pupils now growing to the size of acorns.

There is hunger in his stare, and it scares me. I've seen this look from the men Lollie unintentionally seduces, although she never reciprocates it. It's an animalistic look that must link back to a time when primal urges were all we were. It's been so long since I've kissed anyone, and he seems like the best candidate in this situation—in any situation for that matter.

Our gazes don't waver. He licks his lips, and for a moment I almost lean forward. My hands brace the brick wall of the bar behind me. The moon-colored rings around his irises shimmer. It's a bewitching reaction, and it does the trick to pull me out of whatever is happening between me and this stranger. I manage to get my wits about me and put some space between us.

"What's your name?" I ask. He brushes his knuckle to his nose, then flashes a smile that is full of secrecy, his eyes darting to the bar door. My eyes follow.

"What the hell are you doing out here, Jade? You've been gone forever." Lollie asks and grabs my tense hand with her relaxed one.

"I thought you were following me out, and so I was just talking to…" I look around, but there is no one. The man had just been right in front of me. A frustrated sigh escapes my mouth, realizing what has just happened. One of my overly imaginative daydreams—again.

I've been cursed with them since childhood. Most I can brush off, but some, like the one that just occurred, set me back quite a bit, and I have a hard time regrouping myself after. Never has one involved an actual face, though. A face that seemed to look right into my darkest desires and blur the lines of reality and dreams.

Most would think he ducked into the bar when they weren't looking, but I know it wasn't reality. A man has never shown me so much as an ounce of interest, not because of the way I look, but because of my fuck-off demeanor. Except, I have now found myself questioning that mindset twice today.

I look at Lollie and open my mouth to speak, still a bit in shock. It must be close to one in the morning by now. The street that stood desolate just mere moments before is filled with bar goers walking along the sidewalks. Confusion sets deep in my bones, but I do my best to ignore it.

Whenever I get these types of unexpected visions, I think of the line from that one Fleetwood Mac song about keeping them to myself, and that is just what I do. I shove them into a locked part of my mind, hoping they will never see the light of day again.

"I'm ready to go home," Lollie says. I look back at her, my head spinning and more than happy to hear those words from my dear friend. Linking my arm in Lollie's, we set our sights on a cab.

"Yeah, me too," I breathe out, looking forward to the comfort of my bed.

The cab ride seems to drag on forever. The temptation to spill every detail to Lollie about both men from today is weighing like a bag of bricks over my head. Both having no names, and one quite possibly being a figment of my imagination.

I thank my heavy tongue for staying quiet as we both make our way out of the cab. An added benefit of living just a block away from each other. My mind is fuzzy and tired, thinking only of curling up in my queen-sized bed and pulling my periwinkle blue comforter up to my chin.

I walk Lollie to her door, my embrace squeezing her sides a little longer than normal. There is a lot to be said about a hug that is meaningful, and the ones between Lollie and me always are.

"I'm glad you came out tonight, Jade. Oh, and just so you know, I'll be over banging on your door in the morning with muffins from the corner shop. You can thank me now." She says the last bit with an exaggeration that makes me giggle. I truly hope she isn't drunk talking because a warm blueberry muffin from our favorite morning cafe sounds too good to be true right about now.

"I'm counting on it. But not *too* early," I squint at her. She sticks her tongue out at me and walks into her small Tudor home.

Once I hear the click of her lock, I make my way across the street, passing the small magnolia tree Lollie planted when she first moved in. The glow from the streetlights is a strange comfort I'll never get bored with. Casting off shadows in the distance that would normally send a young woman the other way.

My eyes bend the shadows to meld giant outlines of men with tree branches bursting from their temples and roots for hands. Anyone in their right mind would quicken their step to a faster speed, but I walk on at a wobbly ease.

Being on the second floor has its perks, but I don't see any of those right now as I lean against the railing and slowly make my way up. I applaud myself once I am finally past the front door of my apartment, peel off my shoes and fill a glass of water three times before I feel hydrated enough to make it to my bed. I don't even bother taking off my makeup as I crawl longingly under its lush comforter.

Between the walls moving around me from the alcohol, and the overthinking going on in my mind from one of the strangest days of my life thus far, hot sweats take over my skin making my heart beat rapidly in my chest. It's an uncomfortable feeling, having this unknowing of what my life is about to become. Caught between what I've known and what I will.

My thoughts reach into the depths of the memory of my mother, hoping she can guide me in the right direction. But she is no longer here, so it is a pointless hope. When my heart does finally calm, and I think I might make it through to see this day end, I can't seem to shake the feeling of foreboding. My only thought being that today has opened a world of trouble, starting with the moment the jade willow tree shattered. Leaving me with a ring, a house, and a gravely gorgeous man whose face I can't seem to get out of my mind.

FLASHBACK
RACINE, LOUISIANA 1860 *
NEW ORLEANS OUTSKIRTS

In a time before I knew such things could exist, I would dream of trees with portals within their roots. Slowly, as I got older, those dreams crept back to me.

It is almost dark when I awaken with the leather-bound book still open in my hands. I snuck the copy of Frankenstein *from my mother's study and must have dozed off beneath the old hickory again. This is a common occurrence for me during these warm days when the sun casts a soft shimmering glow that reaches down through the flickering leaves above.*

The hawk sitting on the branch high over my head looks down upon me, utterly annoyed that I am here yet again. However, I am unconcerned with his skeptical glare, because while I have spent many days here in the recent weeks, I know he has no one to tell. My secret is safe amongst the hawk's hard and discerning eyes.

Whispers swarm around me like summer gnats at my face, but there is no one to cast them. My head rests on the dark, soft moss-covered ground, while my eyelashes flutter up to one of the giant tree roots sitting above the surface as if it were a talon and everything beneath it were its prey.

I grasp the large claw-like root jumping out of the soil with my still sleepy hand. I can barely wrap my small, slender fingers around it, but use it as an anchor to move to my knees, bending my head down toward the muffled voices within the silky, moss-filled earth.

Leaning into a small hollow at the base of the tree, the whispers get louder, and I almost feel as if I can see a glimmer of light beneath. But how could that be? I lean in to prop my ear against the opening, hoping the otherworldly words will become clear. I have no such luck. Instead, my hand slips against the loose dirt.

Within seconds I am consumed in darkness, and the feeling of falling has me in its deathly grip. I claw at roots, at air—scrambling for anything that might catch me. Nothing holds.

My nails dig deep into the attached roots, but the roots release from the soil, and then they too follow me down into the void. Damp earth assaults my nose. Dirt-caked streaks smear my lace dress as I tumble deeper into the dark. My mother will not be pleased.

Suddenly, my bottom meets a very solid floor. The landing makes my head hurt as I sit and wait for the stars to pass. When I feel steady enough to catch my breath, I move to a crawling position, pressing my palms to the hard ground.

Where am I, I wonder? Tiny scrapes line my fingernails and make appearances up to my elbows. It is cold and damp under my small hands and definitely of an earthly texture.

A faint light pokes through a large rectangular structure wedged between two deep taproots. I inch closer to see, using dangling roots hanging above to pull myself to my feet. The space is tight. Roots brush along my shoulders like luring fingers. I see what the structure is now, although I almost don't believe it.

It is a door. A door forged within some sort of warren under a very large tree that I had a very different perspective of just a few moments ago. How something man-made came to be under a hickory tree is not something most can process, and I have trouble doing so myself.

Curiosity gets the best of me, and I move closer to reach for the knob. It is a heavy green stone, and I turn it slightly. The light moves across the earth, casting an illuminating shadow as I expose what is behind—a world under the world I've known all my life.

Tiny bulb-like lights float around the earthen burrow, mimicking fireflies on a summer night. If I could catch one, I would swear it was a small being in human form radiating light from within. Shimmering black and gold insects skitter to hide into deep crevices along the dirt walls as I pass by. I am grateful for the vast openness all around that welcomes me, much different from the hollow on the other side of the door I just stepped through.

Another door comes into view, made entirely of the same green stone. I wish I could put a name to it because I know I have seen it before. Perhaps, a paperweight in my mother's study? I put my hand to it, feeling a jolt of electricity flowing from my fingers through the surface of the door in a swirl of sparkles.

It is almost as if this threshold, as if this new realm is reacting to me, but how is that so? My hand shimmers against it still, trans-forming my whole body in a sunlit sheen. The door releases, opening to two vibrant blue-green orbs. Oh, I have seen these before.

"Finally opening your eyes, sweet succulent," a dark deep voice rumbles.

I attempt to catch my breath as I sit up abruptly and plant my hands upon soft, pillowy moss, which I now realize feels more like my blanket. I tighten it into a ball, making sure a blanket is indeed what I am touching. Those familiar eyes peer through the darkness at me, turning into the street lamps I see out my bedroom window.

I imagine the eyes again, matching them to the man who paid a visit to my shop just yesterday. But why would I dream of him, apart from the obvious? I brush my dark copper-colored locks away from my face and let myself fall back onto my pillow. That didn't feel like a dream. It felt real and, even worse, it felt known.

My nightgown damp with sweat clings to places I'd rather it not. I jostle out of the bed, leaving the lingering whispers no one to reach. It is five in the morning, and the sink feels miles away. I splash cold water against my face, but my nostrils only take in the scent of damp earth—a smell I'm becoming very familiar with. A fragrance only the roots of the hickory know.

4

FOREVER FRIENDS

DETROIT 1978

I sit in my shop after another not so busy afternoon. The urge to move plagues my spirit. Pacing in circles around the near-ancient findings is all I can do, my mind a chaotic mess. Carya peeks from behind a hulking amethyst geode, her yellow eyes flickering with unease.

By no means am I an anxious person, but something has switched within me. The moment the jade willow shattered, and the ring touched my skin, I knew something had shifted. As if the Gods had handed me a path and dared me to follow it. The man and the dream last night eating at my subconscious. A vibration within my marrow screaming at me to pay attention.

The jumpy feeling within me eases once Lollie comes by looking worse than I do. Huge brown sunglasses cover her tired eyes as she stands before me in tan bell bottoms and a random cropped band t-shirt. Her hair swept up in a long and messy, barely made braid.

She is a free spirit, and it shows in her wardrobe. Where my everyday wardrobe comprises items that are organized and structured, she wears whatever will make her stand out the most. I look at her with sincerity and relief. She is just the excuse I needed.

"Oh, thank goodness, Lol. Let's go get a coffee and walk through the park. I am dying for some air." She reluctantly pulls her body out of the musty leather chair tucked in the shop's corner that she had just collapsed into.

"Do I have to?" She groans. Last night was rough for both of us. And while I seem to have recovered just fine, it is obvious Lollie has not.

"No, but I'm drowning in my thoughts. Come on, I'll even throw in a muffin from the bakery, remember the ones *you* were going to bring me this morning..." I do my best to persuade her. She can be stubborn as a bull when she wants to be.

"Ugh. Fine. But if I throw it all up, I'm blaming you." She moves forward, dragging her feet like a dismissive teenager.

"Deal." I pull her close and loop my arm through hers.

We leave the bakery with our pastries and coffees, and we walk silently through the park. Lollie, who isn't her usual talkative self, looks up at the trees the whole time. I sense her mind working behind her wide-framed sunglasses.

"Are you sure you want to take on all this new house stuff right now?" She says after a deep breath. "It seems like it came on so fast. You don't have to go right away; you can stay here in the city...with me." She nervously spins the creamy white stone ring that adorns her finger, flashes of iridescence catching my eye.

"Aw, Lol, are you going to miss me?" I smirk at her jokingly, but then it quickly drops when I look into her eyes that hold the tears she is trying to keep back. I take her hands in mine as her worry seeps into them. Her emotions swimming in a muddled river to me. There really isn't much I can say that could ease her mind, so I decide to go with the truth.

"I *have* to go. I need to figure out why this has been placed in my lap," I shrug. I know it's not what she wants to hear, but it needs to be said. "If I don't go now, it'll be all I think about until I do." Lollie looks down at our hands. Still toying with her ring with a silent regard.

"What if you don't like the reason why?" she whispers. I'm taken aback by her unsteady voice that won't let this go. Her comment is unwanted because I feel I am doing the right thing. Something is pulling me there, and it gets stronger by the day.

"I mean," she continues with a little more pep in her words, "just don't go finding any new best friends on me or fall in love with some backwards-talking Southern guy." She winks, but when she looks at me again, she is all business. I give her the biggest hug, so grateful that I have her to worry about me.

"Never," I say. But I'm not too sure about the second part, because as I hug her, a certain someone with branches tattooed against his arms pops up in my mind's eye.

The walk back is quiet, but handing Lollie the key sparks a new reform in me. I give her the rundown of the shop upkeep, and an idea of what the average workday around here looks like. Her eyes glaze over by the time I finish explaining, her not-so-subtle disappointment shining between blinks.

She is very much aware of how to run this shop, since she's covered for me more than a couple of times when I was sick. And then when my mother passed and the days after when I couldn't bear to get out of bed. Although on those days, she would usually just crawl in bed with me, and the shop would just stay closed.

I peck Lollie on the cheek as she takes off to sleep off her hangover, most likely for the rest of the day. A new excitement fills me as I rummage through the papers left here from the man with sea-foam eyes. His name is still a mystery, partly because I haven't wanted to look for it. I am still trying to push away the reaction I had when he set foot in my shop.

The remnants of the jade willow tree are still piled up on the counter by the register, and I pull the ring from it again. Pinching it between my pointer and my thumb, I'm drawn to the intrinsic beauty of this thing. It holds such detail that it could only have been made by hand. And when you look closely at the stone pieces cradled inside the welded metal, they are fragmented as if they too were tiny pieces broken off from a much larger stone. Did my mother know the ring was in here? She couldn't have. Although my mother always loved a good mystery.

It's then that I decide the ring will be coming with me to Racine. In fact, I feel more relaxed with it in my hand as I close a fist around it. My breath snags, a sudden ache blooming where longing and fear tangle like roots beneath my constricted ribs. Forcing my will, I open my fist and put the ring in my coat pocket. It helps the feelings dissipate—a little. A temporary fix to a problem I don't understand in the least bit.

The pressure of packing nagging at my brain, I make a quick decision to leave early. Keeping the small orange dome-shaped lamp on for Carya, but turning off the rest of the lights. I hope she appreciates the cozy gesture.

The air is still when I finally lock up the front door. Ashton's pub bustles with the sound of chatter, showing no signs of closing early. A good sign for someone who works as hard as he does.

I walk fast enough that the city sounds fade out of my earshot, and then my only focus is to get home. I don't even register the faint rustling whisper of oak leaves weaving through my hair.

I make my way to my door, then to my room. An itch creeps along my spine that I know something about the jade ring. About the hickory. But what is it?

Only in sleep does my mind awaken, and the feelings I've buried rise like fog—formless but pressing.

My dreamy head is a blur of feathers. One set is iridescent black, and the other is a glittering golden brown. As they move farther from my vision, it looks as if two birds are dancing. A poetic waltz of wings and beaks. But as I look longer, their talons tell a different story. They are not dancing in synchronicity, but battling in a chaotic duel of blood and fury.

Two trees stand tall in the background, looking almost human.

The arm-like limbs connected to the powerful bodies of bark sway as if orchestrating the whole thing. The birds being puppets of the trees' bidding.

Something within the fighting bird's talons breaks free and falls, bouncing a couple times before settling at my feet. It is the jade ring, glowing with an electric pulse that grabs my attention. I lean down, my fingertips registering its energy before brushing the shiny metal.

A sharp prick.

Pulling my finger back in response, I see the ring has morphed into some sort of purple flower. Tiny spiked thorns rimmed the long, slim and delicate mass of petals like the collar of an evil queen protecting her ageless beauty. Blood drips steadily from my finger, forming a small puddle that slowly spreads across the ground.

Soon my blood is filling the ground. I can't stop it. I spot the ring again sinking into the dark red liquid. It falls deeper, and deeper still. I try to reach for it, but my arm is slowly being coated in a mix of blood and dirt. Thick wooden cords coil around my waist like muscle. I thrash, desperate for air. It is no use. I take one last breath as I too am lost to the earth, tangled within roots that refuse to let me go. And they never will.

$$5$$

BIRDS

DETROIT 1978

Morning comes quickly, and it seems not to care at all that I would like it to slow down. It is my last day in Detroit. My last day as a youngish, naïve antique shop owner. In one day's time, I will add estate owner to my resume, and I'm not entirely sure how I feel about that title.

My black suede thigh-high boots click against the sidewalk as I make my way to the place I feel most at home. This shop of mine has provided a cocoon where I would happily slumber in an oblivious wake state through the years, but with little warning, it seems now I am meant to transform. To embrace something different. Something down south, beckoning me to it more and more since finding out it could be mine.

The day is breezy and warm, making my pleated chiffon skirt cling to the front of my thighs. The back sways out behind me like leaves of a willow billowing in the breeze. Willows were always my mother's favorite tree, but the only glimpse I've had of one lately is the jade willow statue sitting in a hundred odd-shaped pieces on my shop counter.

There were many willows at the lake we lived near before coming to Detroit, and perhaps that is why my mother was so reluctant to leave. The reason we came here was never quite clear to me then. Young minds often miss the reasons for things, but they tend to feel the big picture, regardless. And I know the reason we left that lake was important. My mother had fear written all over her face that day she packed everything in the car.

I round the corner of the block to make it onto Sixth Street, and I'm just about knocked over by a heady dark floral aroma. A small oak near my shop looks weighed down by a mass of black leaves. This constant smell always lingers around this oak, but where else have I smelt this? As I inch closer, I see the leaves are actually an iridescent blue-black, and are not actually leaves at all. They are feathers. Crow feathers.

The oak sits heavy with crows, every beady eye fixed on me. They weigh on the tree and on my spirit. An ominous and sensual feeling sweeps through me. Not feeling comfortable in my skin, I aggressively shove my key in the door, breaking a nail in haste, and all but jump in to get rid of the feeling of being watched.

Once the door is closed, the welcome meow of Carya eases my nerves, and only then do I release the breath I've been holding since realizing what occupied that poor distressed oak. When did I get a starring role in an Alfred Hitchcock movie? I sweep my fingers along Carya's back, my hand shaking from the eerie impression those birds left me with.

Carya meows once more and brushes against me, as if she knows I'm on edge. She has been acting strangely ever since the estate lawyer came by. I can't say I blame her. My constant shadow these last couple of days, weaving in between my legs and testing my acrobatic abilities. She doesn't seem to want to leave my side, so it is then that I decide to take her with me to see my newly inherited mansion.

The day carries on like any other before my inheritance, a quiet pressure building within me. If you looked at this day as an outsider, you would think nothing of it. No show of outward distraction, but from my view it looks as if everything has been set ablaze. Ripe with anticipation of the next part of my journey. After all, all monumental change starts from within. I just wish mine had a clearer focus.

The door chimes, which sets my nerves on edge, but I'm greeted by a comforting smile. Ashton places a steaming bowl of brown soup in front of me from the local deli, the blue and red design on the carryout bowl giving it away. It's rather warm outside for soup, but once the brothy aroma reaches me, I'm left with no choice but to see if its taste matches its mouthwatering smell.

Jumping from my stool and giving Ashton a quick peck on the cheek, I sit cross-legged on the floor with it. Ashton automatically mirrors my actions. He joins me with his own meal as we eat on the floor, discussing the many plans I have yet to decide on.

"Jade, you are too pure of heart. And that is such a good thing, but not down there. There is so much injustice down there...I would hate for you to be hardened because of it," Ashton says. The worry consumes his words. I can tell from his posture he seems reluctant for me to go.

He fears I won't mix well with the people in the southern states. My mind has always been more liberated than most, and I have a hard time seeing unjust behavior toward anyone based on their color, gender, or societal ranking. My mother is to blame for that conviction, and I've heard no one complain about it until now.

"Ash, I'll be fine. If anyone needs to worry, it's you. How will you manage Lollie while I'm gone?" I push his shoulder, and he smirks knowingly.

"Nobody can manage *her*," the words fall out with a twinkle in his eye. I tumble back into a fit of giggles, almost sending my soup bowl across the room. I swear Ashton tries, but fails to hide his version of blushing. His cheeks, normally tawny brown, turn a deep color of pink. Why he reacts this way has me curious, but I can't control my laughter enough to ask.

He and Lollie ended in a way I think Ashton rather forget.

Ashton, head over heels in love, took Lollie to The London Chop House. The nicest restaurant in Detroit.

I was sure Ashton had plans to make their relationship official, at least it seemed that way with how he pulled on his necktie and kept messing with his hair, waiting for Lollie to finish getting ready. I was over at Lollie's beforehand, helping her choose her outfit, so I got to see firsthand the seriousness of this dinner. It was comical really—until it wasn't.

Lollie called me in tears a couple of hours later, saying they were over and he would never see life the way she does. That was all I heard about it from both of them, but I didn't pry. The feelings from them being of almost atomic bomb proportions had me nervous to detonate an already very unsteady tension.

Both have seemed to calm around each other since then, being that was almost two years ago. I left them with little choice but to see each other almost daily, even if they barely spoke for that first year after. Lollie is my oldest friend, but Ashton's heart holds so much value. Neither was going anywhere out of my life.

Ashton always seems to know when I need someone around. Today being one of them. His sun-kissed hair falls behind his ears and curls up a bit. And his smile is so wide and gleaming that it never fails to break my heart right open.

He is the optima of light, and that light dimmed when he and Lollie ended. Even dimmed, his light is a solar flare—igniting energy the moment he steps into a room. He came into my life as a friend from the moment he opened up shop across from ours, and he is one I hope never to lose.

Ashton leaves after finishing his food, his visits being short since having to carry the responsibility of his shop. The rest of the day at the shop is quiet, per usual. My heart tugs a bit at knowing I'm going to miss this comfortable routine of shop life. One thing I've never been too keen on is taking chances, and this house feels like the biggest one of all.

This shop life is all I've known. My mother cast a shadow of fear over anything I ever dared to try. I know she didn't mean to, but why was she so afraid? It's no wonder I unconsciously picked up her unhealthy pattern over the years, as so many young children do.

Maybe the house, tossed into my hands like a dare, could be how I finally break the generational curse. To embrace the change that's always stirred in me. To climb the tree of life without the dreaded fall to the ground that I have for so long expected as the only outcome.

I stay at the shop for one last night to clean it up and listen to records with Carya, a glass of cherry brandy in hand. With my liquor poured and the record player set to *One of These Nights* by the Eagles, I get into a steady rhythm of taking stock of what is in the shop.

I slowly brush my fingers along the edge of a painting dating back to the mid-nineteenth century of a young woman submerged in a lily pond fully dressed. My mother found it in Europe years ago before I was born, and I've always thought it looked like someone I knew. At times, I saw my very own face in the woman's reflective melancholy staring up in quiet contemplation.

"Why so sad, beautiful girl?" I would often ask as if she weren't just mere paint strokes on canvas.

My thoughts wander back to the estate and the uncle I never knew. The irony that my uncle was an antique collector is not lost on me, and it's what stirs my curiosity the most. Would he own items as timeless as these paintings? I have spent my whole life surrounded by the odds and ends of items from different ages, and now I wonder if perhaps it has been rooted in my blood all along.

As if my mind conjures it with the very word itself, a dense black door with pictures of various trees engraved in it floods my vision, pouring in from an unknown source. I can pick out the hickory and oak carved larger and darker than the rest. A hawk glides above the hickory, while one lonely crow sits perched atop the oak etching. It's beautiful detail entrancing me into it's imagined world.

I put my hand on the knob, about to turn it, but pull back instinctively with the feeling of something slick and warm seeping onto my fingers. My hand now covered in a dark red color that is slowly creeping up my arm in an act defying the natural order of the earth's gravitational pull.

I catch movement on the door. The hawk and the crow become lifelike, growing before me. The hawk swooping down at the crow. The crow heading right toward my head. I open my mouth to scream, but before the scream falls on empty air, I am brought back to the present time. Back in my shop. The beating wings of the birds still pulsing in my ears.

I grip the counter, fingers digging into the wood. It threatens splinters, but my frantic heart pays no heed. Forcing steady breaths through my lips, I find the stool to steady my legs and my heart, both are leaving me with little support. My fingers still feel the wet thickness of blood.

My visions have been getting worse. What were dream-like states that graced my mind every few months has now turned into a daily occurrence. I can't help but recognize that whatever I am about to embark on has a lot to do with it.

6

THE DRIVE

DETROIT TO RACINE 1978

The day of my departure grips me like a hawk to its prey, taking me to some unknown destination, whether I like it or not. Thankfully, and to no surprise, Ashton lets me borrow his car for the drive down to Louisiana. He's loaded the trunk with snacks and emergency supplies in case of a flat tire, or God knows what else he thinks is an emergency. Sometimes I wonder what he wouldn't do for me.

It can be a burden to be surrounded by people who want to protect you so fiercely. If I were a delicate rose, I think my petals would surely crinkle beneath that pressure. Though I would be lying if I said I never felt that way. And now here I am, comparing myself to a flower.

The more I think about it, I've always found the thorns on a rose a funny addition. So far from its flowering bud that any animal could surely nip the most alluring part without being snagged by the thorns in the slightest. The thistle from my dream would be more of a flower I would like to mimic. Its petals untouchable and bold. Saying, "Here I am, but good luck taking what's mine."

However, I don't feel any burden from Ashton's friendly deed at the moment as he hands me the keys, and makes traveling miles and miles to a destination I know nothing about, a whole lot easier. I thank him a million times before I load up the fairly new blue station wagon he spent years saving up for.

My anxiety has me biting my nails down to the nubs as I think about even getting so much as a scratch on it. To say my driving is dependable is an exaggeration. I've had no need to drive where we live, and it shows.

It shows in my nervous fingers as I fondle the keys, wondering how something so small could be so dangerous when put in the wrong hands. It shows on Ashton's anxious face mixed with the hopeful energy that I won't crash his pride and joy. And worst of all, it shows in my driving, or lack thereof.

Ashton reminds me he's coming down with Lollie in three months to retrieve it once I know at least one car left to me at the estate works. Lollie is hovering beside me, her perfume smelling like a sweet spring morning. I turn, giving her the tight embrace I so desperately need, holding in the tears that sting the back of my eyes.

When I let her go, I see she is in a similar shape, but tears are already free-falling down her cheeks. These last few days have brought on the waterworks for both of us. I use the back of my hand to wipe the dampness I feel moving down to my chin. Tears are treacherous little things. When they choose to fall, they do as they please, whether or not for the right reason. This is the right reason.

In all my years of knowing Lollie, I don't think we have ever been apart for more than a couple of days, let alone three months. We even went to all our summer camps together growing up, and I remind myself that she too will be down to visit come October.

"Don't forget we are here, Jade," she voices. Lollie's eyes are sharp and serious in this moment. I can feel her friendship strongly through that look. "For anything. Don't forget."

"I won't, Lol," I say in response. I give her my best attempt at a smile, hoping it reassures her. "It's only a little time away. We'll be together again before you know it." I hope the words I choose are what she wants to hear, being our last words face to face and all.

I pop Carya in the passenger seat and close the door before she can glide her way out of the car. Her slinky body curls up, gazing out the window like she knows what she's leaving behind. I have no idea how she will do on the car ride, and I'm not eager to find out.

Lollie blows me a kiss as I back away from the drive, and I stick my arm out the window, waving goodbye to both her and Ashton. Ashton's hands in his pockets, his eyes trail the back headlights. Lollie stands with her arms hugging herself, tears still glistening on her face.

I curse the traffic and ease into the slow lane to let some of the impatient drivers pass by, still trying to catch glimpses of my musing friends in the rearview mirror. I look back at the oak that was full of crows the day prior and breathe a sigh of relief that there is not one in sight. First good omen of the trip.

After that, the hours after fly by. Once I find my groove in the driver's seat, I'm feeling rather proud of the time I've made, and the absence of accidents on my part. My hands keep a tight grip on the wheel as we make it into Nashville, and I give myself an imaginary pat on the back. The map that sits crinkled in my lap says this marks the halfway point. In less than eight hours, I'll be in uncharted territory and completely way over my head.

"Almost there, Carya." I look at my sweet feline companion, feeling insanely blessed to have her presence.

I turn up the dial on the radio. Queen blares through the speakers and sends a lively buzz through my hair along with the wind blowing through the halfway rolled-down window. I do my best to hit the high notes, which gets me a very unamused and concerned look from Carya. The sun hits her just right, so she becomes a warm, amber glow.

I'm of the mindset that this adventure may be just what I need. Michigan has been the only place I've belonged since I was a child.

In the summers, we would travel to the east coast, but never went below Kentucky.

My mother would always give some excuse about the weather being too warm down south, but secretly, I knew she was avoiding the subject of my father. From what I have deciphered from the few things she has said about him, he is from one of the southern states. Her tight lips about the matter were all I needed to know that some things hurt too much to talk about.

I dip my head forward, peering out the front windshield to get a glimpse of the blue cloudless sky. Above my car, I see the most magnificent rusty brown hawk. Soaring and keeping a watchful eye on the road. I remember the hawk that sat on that old hickory from my youth—always watching. Holding both pride and protection within its cream-hued breast.

The one I see now is fairly high in the sky, and although it doesn't look large from my perspective, I can tell the wingspan is one that would do well enough to carry off Carya if she weren't fast asleep in my lap. The beauty of the way it soars effortlessly, as if it were made of sky and cloud, brings me to a place of content and longing.

I continue to coast through an ever-changing landscape. My car roams through green hills that morph into roads that zig and zag through edgy mountains leading to valleys with cities full of lights. I drive out of one of those cities now as the looming night creeps upon the sky. The hawk is long gone, but its guidance provided an imaginary safe passage to where I hope to near soon.

The map crunches in my grip as I scan the colored lines on the paper trying to find the road to the estate. There are no marked roads on the map to lead me to the house. I keep driving deep into a more wooded, secluded path that leads to a dead end. A path of tall trees lines all my sides apart from a small opening that must have been a private drive at some point. I take a chance, an action I have slowly been getting more comfortable with since this week started.

The road is unmarked, and the entrance to the drive is covered in brambles. I cringe when I think of Ashton's car scratching along their prickers. I get out of the car, inhaling the warm southern air. The evening hangs heavy as I do my best to push most of the spindly shrubs away.

My hands are left littered with tiny cuts from the thorns, not the most welcoming sign. I keep pushing them out of the way, trying to clear a decent path. Hidden within the brush are purple thistles that I recognize from my dream just mere days ago.

A humming within my chest makes me aware of the ring inside the pocket of my jean coat located just atop my heart. A ring could not leave such sensations. It must be nerves making my heart race as much as my mind is in this moment. I pat my pocket gently. Still there.

I turn down the drive, and it opens a bit with beautiful cypress trees lining the drive. Spanish moss hangs from their branches listlessly, like they have nothing better to do but lounge in the dimming late July sun. The driveway lasts a full ten minutes, and it seems to have been a little better kept the further I make my way in.

I sigh in relief as I'm greeted by a bronze and white sign, *The Rooted Realm Estate*. My risk paid off, and I smile with satisfaction at my decision. The interesting name shows its true meaning right away. There are trees lining every inch of this acreage.

A valley of vast oaks to my left. Cypress, pines, and cherry trees line the right, and the largest hickory I think I have ever seen sits in its own respective nook in the back of the property. These trees all seem eager by the way their roots push to the surface like worms after a fresh rain.

In awe, I stop my car. The engine slows to a soft purr before I turn it off and step out cautiously. I follow the circle drive holding Carya in one arm, and carry my suitcase in the other, which is challenging to say the least. Carya is a ball of motion trying to skirt her way out of my grip, but I barely notice because I am overcome by all that my eyes are taking in.

A massive Acadian old white house stares back at me sitting up on a slight hill. A dark pink cast of color sits across it, weaving into its window panes from the soon to be sleeping sun as she finally trades off with the glow from the waxing moon. An odd magnolia tree sits off to the side of a wraparound open porch. There are twelve deep steps to make their way up to the front door, which seems excessive, but the house itself looks built up as if the bottom level is halfway above ground.

I am eager to see what is held behind these doors. Doors that are full of the most ornate designs carved into the heavy wood with old worn copper gates embedded within them. The doors are calling to me, much like the old hickory from my old childhood home did. I answer their call immediately and move forward, drawn by the strange pull of the house, as if it already knows me.

7

THE HOUSE

RACINE 1978

It is a house made from my dreams, seeming to belong to my soul before I even stepped inside. And the moment I step inside, I am transported to a time before. A time of luxury and quality. When people made things with their hands linked firmly to their heart's intent.

The floors are set in a rich wood, full of character that holds the memories of each step that has worn its path along these halls. I flick on a large lamp sitting on a table by the door, grateful the electricity wasn't turned off after my uncle's passing. The light shines brightly, so I can see all that is before me.

The stairway that leads to the upper floor almost takes up the whole entryway. There is a large mirror on the wall to the right and a massive brass chandelier. Both the mirror and the chandelier seem to have been created from a fury of leaves. I've seen nothing like it, but they pull me in like a siren song as I drop my bags at my feet.

Carya is still in my arms, and I watch her hesitantly explore as I set her down. She seems just as entranced as I am. I sweep my hand across the mirror's moldings. It seems older than the house itself. Everything else in the house is an eclectic mix of all the eras of time, except the mirror. Generations of treasures marked in time, but this mirror, it seems archaic, having no time my mind can date it back to, looking like it's from a different world altogether.

Its reflection shows how my hair falls limply behind my back. The drive here did it no justice. Coffee stains litter my oversized t-shirt from the moments when Carya couldn't get comfortable, and I had to juggle the steering wheel and my cup. I should think I look a mess, but when I look in this mirror, I feel anything but.

In fact, a strange feeling of being watched brushes across my skin, as if someone were within looking out. I skate my fingers along my neck and watch my reflection mirror the motion, unsure why I feel seen. I drop my hand *and* my silly notions as I let out an exhale. If someone were on the other side, they must see how ridiculous I feel now.

Tucked between the stairs and the kitchen, there is a large black door. Upon opening it, a gust of wind nearly knocks me over as I look down into deep-set concrete steps. The gust brings with it a stench of damp earth and roots, drenching me immediately. It is definitely a basement, which seems odd for a state that is mostly below sea level. Looking deeper down sends chills that curl around my spine and travel up my neck. I slam the door shut without thinking.

It is then that I focus on the now closed door, and the markings engraved throughout its stained wood. Markings that spark something in me when I brush my hands over them. My fingertips brush over the varieties of trees with roots that all connect toward the bottom of the door. A door from my vision.

Never have my visions played out in real life, and never have I thought any of them had meant anything. I take a shaky step back and decide I will not go any further. My only thought now is to explore the less creepy parts of this mansion.

Everything about this house is old and ethereal, with touches of vintage charm and secret nooks everywhere. Even the walls seem to whisper of a time and place far away, when masquerade balls were a common occurrence and people dressed in gowns made from fabrics of silk and brocade. A time much different from now, but you can still feel its presence amongst the rooms of this estate. What secrets were kept behind its lush luxury?

I find it fascinating that parts of this house call to the comforts of my soul, while others seem to repel it. Or could the repulsion be fearful energy from moments occurring from the owners before?

My mother would often talk about a residual energy that can be felt by the body, but not seen by the eyes. She told me always to heed its warning. This week has been the first time I've ignored her advice.

I venture upstairs with my luggage. Dark brown wood makes up the steps leading to the top, and the banister has the same leaf and tree design deeply engraved into it as the mirror. In my explorations, I've found that there are six baths and seven rooms altogether. Way too much house for only one man. Who else walked these halls?

The three bedrooms upstairs are bright and welcoming. I pick the one with a view of the small pond connecting to the swampland. Looming cypress trees cover the swamp, hiding what lurks beneath. Carya would make a nice snack for whatever is out there. I cringe at the thought.

Looking out the window, I see what really lured me to this room. A willow. A strong, loving presence moves through it in the way its long wispy branches sweep across the surface of the pond. To me, its branches look like a warm blanket, and I am immediately set at ease.

This room comforts me, and I can't help but be reminded of my mother. I see her now in my mind's eye dipping her toes in a moonlit lagoon, toying with the leaves of a willow branch between her fingers, a warm but fractured smile on her lips.

Within the roots your answer lies, she whispers to me.

I blink and am brought back into the bright sunny bedroom, processing if I truly just heard my mother's voice. Trying to regain my equilibrium, I sit on the edge of the bed. My flashes of 'insight' are at an all-time high, and I'm having a hard time sorting through all that they have to say.

My mother's soft whisper within my subconscious reminds me of a time she had said something similar in her last days on this earth. Her unknown sickness made her weaker and weaker every day. In her liminal state, she would often tell me of her need to go back to her roots or that she would soon be there anyway. I didn't know what to make of it, and it unsettled me tremendously.

The day she spoke those words, Lollie had told me to take the day off and offered to watch my mother, knowing that seeing her fade away was crushing my soul. But when I returned later that day, they were gone. It wasn't until the evening set that they arrived back. My mother seemed more like herself, while I was a frantic mess wondering where they had been.

"Your mom just needed to get out, so I took her to the old willow she loves in Woodlawn Cemetery," I remember Lollie saying nonchalantly.

I think that was the maddest I had ever been at Lollie, and I did not let her stay alone with my mom again. When she would visit her in her room, I could hear them whispering. In a manner unlike an adopted daughter and mother would have, but more like a sister she had known her whole life.

I would hear only snippets of their conversations before they would notice me lingering by her door. Fragments of phrases like "will protect her" and "in the next life" would flow to my ears, but I did not know what to make of them.

My mother passed just a week later, after her and Lollie's day out. I couldn't help but think the extra exhaustion her body went through that day caused her to pass more quickly. In the end, she was gifted another visit to Woodlawn Cemetery, but this time in the form of ashes mournfully spread along her favorite tree.

I wince as my heart folds into itself, remembering the hardest moment of my young life. I lie back against the bed, and a plush white duvet greets me. The bed cradles me like my mother's touch used to, steady and distant all at once. Sinking in, I let my body relax. This bed doesn't look as if it's been used in decades, but it still holds a coziness that invites me to crawl in. So, I do.

I drift off in this cloud-like bed. My daydreaming does that to me sometimes. The pull of my mind to somewhere else I can't explain makes me sleepy, and most of all confused, because I never seem to understand its meaning. As a child, I would have a few a year. As I've gotten older and especially after the passing of my mother, they've grown in number. These last two weeks, their frequency has gone exponential.

I lock what my mother's voice said in the back of my mind, and give in to the bed's dreamy calling. I hear Carya somewhere in the distance, feeling the comforter around me give way to soft footprints. Only then do I truly fall asleep, while thanking the Gods I brought my orange tabby with to keep me company in this unknown mind fuck of a house.

8

THE VISIT

RACINE 1978

I've spent the last few days looking through the rest of the house. My interest landed in a rickety attic, straight out of an old ghost movie, which seemed to be home to numerous boxes full of antiquities and old letters. I noticed it was also occupied by quite a few spiderwebs. I would have grabbed some boxes down, but the thought of spiders crawling through my hair prevented that outcome completely. So, the boxes stay up there for now, alone and unmoved.

I still haven't ventured to the basement, and I'm not sure I plan to anytime soon. The feeling I felt from it the other day was one I'd rather not revisit. A strange, all-encompassing sensation full of despair is better left unfelt. Especially when I'm already overwhelmed with taking on a new home.

A knock sounds at the door. I quickly turn on the teakettle and make my way to the front room. I called the estate lawyer. You know the one. The one that hasn't left my thoughts since our meeting in my little shop of horrors.

Him—looming above me as if he were going to save me and devour me at the same time. And me—sitting on the floor gazing up at this new stranger, dumbfounded in a pool of my own tears. I'm surprised he would even want to see me again, after such a glorious first impression. However, this is purely professional after all.

I found his number amidst the paperwork he left, along with the name Ry scribbled above it, which looked more like an accidental pen mark. I almost didn't call, thinking perhaps it was not the right man, but the gravelly deep voice that greeted me when he answered the phone was one that is hard to forget.

A voice full of darkness, sin, and danger that seems to release smoke and decay with every word, that also reaches into my feminine existence, calling me to let the wild free. I ache to see the face it's connected to again. My mind can't help but envision twisted sheets and poor decisions with every word he utters, and I want it. But, silly girl, control yourself. You do not even know this man.

My bright smile in greeting is met with a deep scowl from him. Quickly my grin falters, along with the faint desire that was in the pit of my stomach just a minute ago. With a frown, I invite him in, because how can someone be so magnetic and have such a foul disposition at the same time?

"I just put tea on," I say and usher him to the sitting room.

"I don't drink it," he announces curtly. Another lovely remark from the man I just couldn't wait to see again. Perhaps I'll add a little brandy to mine since this is off to such a superb start.

"Well, I do. So, make yourself at home," I say through a strained jaw as I try to bite my tongue from saying anything about his ridiculously rude manner of being.

My hand snatches the book I was reading off the marble side table so he doesn't see it. I found it amidst the lure of the home library this morning. An old book that caught my eye from the moment I set them upon the overloaded sturdy shelves. A book bound in dark green, worn leather with gold embossing. Tattered but speaking of its beauty even after years of being handled by what I can imagine were its many readers. Titled *The Realms Beneath the Roots* with no author to claim it.

An oddity book about ancient tree folklore and the mysterious myths surrounding their origins. The moment I saw its title, I knew I would be reading it in its entirety. I place it off to the side, but I see the lawyer eye its binding, anyway. Thankfully, he says nothing of it. I have so many questions for him, and I hope he will at least be a little more welcoming in his demeanor before I ask them.

I turn on my heels to go fetch the tea, colliding into his hard but comforting chest. He catches me by the elbows, and I look up, wide-eyed and full of surprise. He must think me a clumsy fool the way one side of his mouth curls up, his freshly shaven skin still giving off a hint of the woodsy smelling aftershave he must have put on this morning. I inhale, taking it in while trying to be discreet.

He drops my elbows abruptly, realizing how close we truly are to each other, and within seconds, he has changed. Any smidge of heat from our touch smoldering out into indifference. Apparently, he has the control that I lack. I give a curt apology and scramble to the kitchen in embarrassment, but as I look over my shoulder, Ry stands still, watching my every movement.

Once in the kitchen without his eyes on me, I can breathe. And breathe I do. I attempt to settle the jitters that feel so juvenile right now. The quiet sigh that leaves my lips is met with my regret about calling him. Not because of his less than welcoming attitude, but because of the things I'm experiencing within myself. He's barely been here five minutes and already my nerves are a tangled mess. I want to strip down naked, curse him out, and bare my soul all at the same time.

The teacup and the water glass clink together as I bring them out. Ry is now sitting in one of the green velvet wingback chairs, looking entirely too big for the seat. His elbows rest on his knees with his large hands falling in-between, like he had been waiting an hour instead of mere minutes. He clears his throat.

"About time," he says in the deepest voice that could ever come out of a human.

I ignore his comment because I am completely taken in by the beauty of this man. It is then, as I place the tea on the table between us, that I can really take him in. His dark hair is slicked back, dressed in a dark muted grey fitted suit that barely seems to contain his shoulders.

I again notice markings of the strange tattoos that creep out from behind the cuffs of his jacket. The more I stare at the tattoos, the more I forget the purpose of this visit. Instead of asking him more about the house, I've suddenly become enraptured with knowing only about him.

"So, Ry? Is that short for anything? Ryan? Perhaps you have a last name?" I ask before I lose my nerve. He looks up at me.

"Just Ry. And yes, I have a last name. It is Heart." *Ry Heart.*

"Have you always lived in the New Orleans area?" I ask another question about him, feeling daring.

"Longer than I'd like to admit, actually. But I've lived in my share of other places, too. Not sure I'd consider this town a part of New Orleans, though." He does a quick sweep of me with his eyes and then continues without explaining more,

"So, Jade," my name sounding too natural coming off his lips, "now that you are here, what are your thoughts on the house?"

What are my thoughts on the house? What are my thoughts? My mind is blank as I look abashedly at this beautiful creature before me, but finally I find myself again and conjure up some words.

"Well...honestly...I adore it. This may sound weird, but there is an unknowingness about it that feels like it's just for me." And before I have time to think it through, I add, "In fact—I'm thinking of keeping it after all."

I look at Ry. I can't tell if he holds anger or hope in his eyes. An odd combination that easily goes along with all the other odd experiences I've encountered lately. I surprise myself, though. I hadn't even realized I had come to that conclusion. The thought slipped off my tongue that I hadn't even fully revealed to myself until now. But it is clear—this house is made for me.

Sitting down in the other green velvet wingback across from him, I look from my steaming teacup to his eyes that may or may not be the same color as my name. My gaze roaming to each and then to his mouth. I clear my throat so I can make my next statement without totally losing my train of thought amidst his stare.

"Also, I was hoping you could help and be an advisor of sorts. I don't know the first thing about owning a house of this size. I cannot imagine getting rid of my shop, and I could really use some help to figure out if I can manage both." Before he can answer, I'm quick to add, "And I'll pay you...for your time...of course" I definitely see a hint of surprise in his eyes then.

"I suppose I can." He finally responds after mulling it over. "I will be rather busy until November, so you may need to stay here a while." He looks at me with eyes that hint at a dare. "Or go back. I don't care, but I won't be coming up to that dreadful place you call home again."

The way he says the last line is laughable. A careful request wrapped up in careless indifference. He has made it very clear how he feels about my beloved Detroit. But also, he has a point. To wait here two whole months seems like I will give my shop up to foreclosure in no time. Ry must sense where my mind has traveled, because he quickly adds,

"Have you looked into your uncle's bank records? He was a rather well-to-do man. He had his share of savings that I think would be yours for the taking, being that you are his only surviving kin." He looks at me quizzically after stating something that should have been so obvious.

In all the time I was worried about the house, I didn't even think about any money he may have left. I look up at him, happy for the comment. Happy to think he may be just the man I need for the job.

"I hadn't. Thank you." I smile up at him, and he zones in on it with a clenched jaw. I don't smile often anymore, so it throws me off how natural it feels around him, until the feeling stops and I drop it.

We stand there, not speaking, but staring at each other with an equal amount of curiosity. Then he clears his throat and once again turns to leave as the silence points to the end of our meeting. But I don't want him to leave. Something snags in my chest like an invisible branch that wants to reach out to him. As standoffish as he is, all I can think about is hoping he will stay longer.

"Uh..." I stammer, trying to think of an excuse to keep him near just a few minutes longer. "Would you mind helping me with some boxes?" I blurt out just as his hand goes to the door handle. He stutters in his movements, releasing a breath, as if he were waiting to be asked not to go. At least, that is what I pray.

"What kind of boxes?" He looks at me and cocks his head to the side. A curious look that teases toward something else.

"Oh, just some old boxes from the attic. There are a lot of them. And to be honest, I'm not a fan of spiders or their webs, and all the spiders of Louisiana seem to have taken residence up there." I grin coyly up at him.

His face relaxes as he takes in my comment and lets a light-hearted chuckle past his lips. He then sweeps his hand absentmindedly through his hair, letting down whatever reserve he had—a relaxed version, so different from what he was when I first met him at the door.

It's not butterflies—more like moths, fluttering low and heavy with the dark feelings he stirs in me. There are moments when you know someone may affect you more than you like. And although I don't know it, this is one of them.

"I can help with the junk...and the spiders." He continues interrupting my thoughts with a playful half-grin.

"Junk?" I ask. Everything I saw piled in the cardboard boxes looked like undiscovered treasure. But then again, I own an antique store, which most people may see as someone else's discarded trash.

"Yeah, junk." His voice unapologetic, "I was here just before your uncle passed to look over his assets and saw the boxes full of odds and ends. That's why I recommend an estate sale of sorts. Well, that was before you decided to keep this hellhole." His frank remark causes me to let a chuckle pass, and he looks at me with inquiring eyes. I can see we view this place through very different eyes.

"OK. Right this way, Dorian Gray," I say. The jab being too good to pass up.

The stairs leading up to the attic are all sorts of unsafe. The worn-down middles show not just their age, but also the frequency of use. I take the steps one by one with Ry behind me, breathing in the mix of dust, creaking boards, and a heavy dose of forewarning.

As I make it up to the middle of the steps, I glance behind me. My hair doing its best job of hiding my focus as I aim my gaze his way. His presence behind me pulls at something deep and physical, as if gravity has shifted beneath us. The corner of his mouth lifts slightly. He is actually smiling. I find I am roused by his amusement.

"Please do tell—is something funny?" I question and smile myself. It's nothing I can help, for I have never seen a smile so entrancing.

"Nothing. This just reminds me of something. A bit of déjà vu," he states while staring up at me. A smidge of heat passing between us.

Turning around with more questions than answers, I once again face the attic ahead. But before I can ask my next question, I take the last step up, meeting sticky strands of silk. I gasp as they cling to my face and stumble backward, grasping onto the closest object to keep from falling back, which happens to be Ry's arm.

Almost immediately, I find two hands placed firmly around my waist, cinching around my bare skin as my traitorous shirt rides up under his hands, skin-to-skin contact catching me off guard and sparking a memory. Upon his touch, I see tangled limbs and melding skin. A woman's hand—no my hand, wearing a jade ring and trailing her fingers along forearms marked like the bark of a hickory tree.

My chest all the way to my cheeks must turn some form of crimson, at least that's what it feels like. A girl bursting into flames from one small graze from this man. I quickly jump out of the firm hands branded with that same bark that seem way too familiar to my skin and scramble up to the attic floor.

"Sorry about that, there...therewasaspiderweb," jumbling all the words together. When Ry doesn't respond, I glance over and am met with those two sea foam eyes looking fierce towards me, his fingers wrapped into tight balls.

Did he feel it too? Or am I imagining all of this? My thoughts are silly and illogical. I pull myself away from his intense inspection and point toward the boxes.

"Well, here they are, like I said. I can grab the smaller ones, and you can start with the two big ones." My voice directs in a breathy manner. I'm debating whether it might be best to play mute, the way my words betray what stirs inside me.

Ry clears his throat and goes for the first giant box, but takes more than a couple of seconds before he moves his eyes away from me. That wasn't real, right? Shaking off the feeling, I keep my head down and start with the work we set out to do.

When we have put all the boxes toward the bottom of the stairs on the second floor, I finally get a look at the attic layout. Apart from the spiderwebs, it is quite cozy. There are built-in shelves along the entirety of the attic, and a small round window towards the back.

Rain from the outside pelts the window as if pleading for my attention. I gaze out at the property. Although blurry from the ever-pounding of raindrops against the glass, the variety of trees seems to be in full view as if perfectly laid out on a map.

The largest tree off to the right by the edge of a wooded area is the hickory. I can see only its giant trunk through the storm, but I decide that will be my next visit. Mostly out of curiosity, and part because my heart feels as if it has an invisible string attached to that tree. Something on the other end tugging me there with all its might.

However, there is another presence I feel all too clearly, and that is the sense of Ry at my back.

"That seems to be all of them," he says, taking a hesitant step towards me. I can feel his warm breath heat the back of my neck, and a glance behind my shoulder tells me he is closer than I think. He could be closer still, and I wouldn't mind. We stand there looking out the small window.

"Do you know the history of this property?" I ask as I look over to him, hoping he won't be staring at me the way he was earlier. Not that I found it uncomfortable. To be honest, it felt quite the opposite.

I would guess most girls would think the same thing looking at him. His megawatt smile that has only made one appearance so far, and his stormy eyes that move like a rogue wave through me.

So much so that my stomach drops to the soles of feet, threatening to stay there until I pick it up and hand it right over to the man. What use of it he would have, I do not know, but I'm starting to think every part of me should be left at his disposal.

"I know little about it, but I know your uncle went out of his way to take excellent care of this property. Toward the end of his life, he spent most of his time walking the property and talking to the trees," he pauses. "And well...that caused some talk around town. The town folk didn't see him much, but they saw enough that they said he had lost touch with reality." He stops, bending down to get a better view of the window, but leaving his mouth mere inches from my ear. "But having met him a few times, I don't believe that to be true. I think he just really loved this land."

"How sad," I whisper, touching the tops of my fingers to my lips in thought.

"Is it though?" Ry surprises me with his response. "To be so content with the earth that you don't feel the need to be affected by outside opinions. To know that nature has its own story to tell, and to be the one to listen as opposed to changing it?" I blush and immediately feel regret over my choice of words. So, Ry is deep. Who knew?

"I mean to say, how lonely. How lonely to feel you only have the trees to talk to." I try to clarify. Ry glances sideways at me, and then looks back out the window before he says,

"Oh, I don't think he was alone at all."

9

RING BOX

RACINE 1978

Ry left shortly after our talk in the attic, leaving me deciphering the comment he made earlier. He had made it seem as if there were no significant other in my uncle's life at the time of his death, and the townspeople seemed to deem him nuts, so how would he not be alone? Was he in fact saying that the trees were his company? While that truly sounds like the makings of a sad poem, I find some solace in it. Knowing that my uncle had a deep connection to nature, much like me.

I grew up attracted to the call of creaking branches in a quiet forest near my childhood home. My thoughts wander to the old hickory tree near the woods on this property, and I dearly hope there will be a break in the rain tomorrow so I can travel out to see what had caught my eye out the attic window.

I am adjusting to the house perfectly, and expect that is because it already felt like home the moment I stepped inside. The quiet knowing of the trees on the property and the house filled my bones with an uncomfortable recognition instantly. Will it always feel like this? Or will this quiet secret it's holding reveal itself in time and leave that part of me at peace?

I unpacked some of the cardboard boxes we had brought down

from the attic earlier in the day. The rectangle containers floppy and breaking apart when I moved them onto a table to shuffle through with more ease. A sure sign of how long they had sat up in that attic unmoved. More old books filled a couple, much like the one that yelled out to me from the library shelves.

One thing I can count on with this rain is the amount of reading it persuades me to do. Not that I've ever needed persuading. Tonight, I look forward to digging into the ancient myths of the trees, hoping I will gain more perspective on my uncle's disposition to this land and the trees that occupy it.

Quite a few of the boxes were overflowing with vintage furs, women's gloves and clip-on earrings that must have dated back to the early nineteen hundreds. More than once, I found myself entranced with the stunning, ornate brooches that were mixed in amongst all the retro magic.

I imagine there must have been a woman in this house at some point. Or multiple women based on the sheer number of feminine accessories. Did my uncle have a love or many in his early days? The inheritance paperwork hinted at no sign of him ever having a spouse, making his mystery grow with every discovery.

Sorting through the miscellaneous but vintage pieces is a sort of therapy. Anytime I hold something that has endured an entire lifetime as someone's property, the energy of sentiment surges through me. The emotions lingering on certain objects, giving me some palpable peek into a past time.

It charges me almost, but there are so many items here that the vibrations feel like ropes securing me to them as if they are mine alone. Still, I continue pulling out items as if it were the only thing I was put here to do.

The evening has quickly fallen into dark night, and the rain remains steady against the expansive roof of the estate. Reaching down to grab the last item at the bottom of the box, I pull out a smaller box, but instead of cardboard it is made of wood. A small trinket box of sorts.

The light brown wood isn't one I recognize, but there is an engraving of interconnected leaves all along it. Arms of a willow branch weave along the smooth surface to what I think is a magnolia flower etched deep within. The clasp, fabricated from an actual branch that looks glazed with some hardened sap, holds the box closed. I pull on it, and it snaps open, breaking the sap as it drops in bits and pieces to the floor.

I slowly open the lid, feeling a weird sense of dread and omniscience at the same time. A cold breeze graces the room from one of the open windows, chilling me to the bone, which is odd for this time of year, even if it is raining.

My gut restricts in a manner that feels all wrong. This box feels wrong. But I open it anyway. My curiosity wins the battle as the lid falls back on its bronze metal hinges. The knots in my stomach grow like rot on a carcass sitting under leaves on the forest floor.

I discover two empty spots inside the box. They look to be nooks to hold some sort of circular object, a ring perhaps. Above one opening, someone marked "Opal" in a beautiful hand-etched script. The name written delicately in a dark reddish-brown ink resembling dried blood. The second compartment is marked Jade, looped in that same dried liquid. Both are empty.

My mind automatically goes to the ring I found within the jade willow tree. That must be a mere coincidence, but I'm having a hard time believing in those anymore. I packed it in my cosmetic case. My bare feet leave vanishing imprints on the floor as I quickly go to retrieve it.

To my relief, the ring is just where I left it. The box in my other hand feels heavy, as if it awaits this transaction in quiet anticipation. Reluctance tries to find me, but I ignore it as I fit the ring inside. A perfect fit. But how? These two worlds of Detroit and this estate keep merging, making my head spin.

I look at my finger wondering if the ring could fit, the buzzy feeling growing stronger and stronger behind my eyes. There are too many coincidences for me to make sense of. The ring hidden in the jade willow now fits perfectly in a box found miles away marked "Jade." And then—there's my name.

Nausea creeps up inside me stronger, urging me not to. My skin hums with a warning I can't ignore. There is a battle within me, my subconscious telling my body yes, but an electricity making itself known all around me to stop. The ring hovers just above the tip as I decide to fight back on the repelling energy around and put it on once and for all.

BOOM!

A bolt of lightning cracks outside, echoing through the house and vibrating up the pads of my feet. I drop the box and the ring, all but jumping out of my skin. The rain must have turned into a storm, and it sounds like a big one at that.

Picking up the box, I secure the ring back inside, saving my curiosity for another day. A feeling of unfinished business works its way into my being. I bury it, like I do so many other things. I doubt it will stay that way.

The wind picks up, and the storm is in full effect by the time I get my bearings. My body moves on autopilot as I start to close the storm windows by securing the metal latches, rain splashing inside the windows and onto my face every time the wind blows.

Being so near the gulf, the house is fitted with huge storm windows and large pull-down guards made from waterproof fabric. I yank down the guards and attach them to the hooks at the bottom of the floor, a feat easier said than done. A rumble of thunder and flashes of lightning breach the open shades of the windows I haven't yet reached. I quicken my movements, hoping the floor isn't completely soaked by the time I'm done.

The last two shades are toward the front of the house. As I walk that way, a pulsing glow reflects off the entry mirror. It must be from one of the windows connected to the adjoining sitting room. I'm about to turn my head that way when without warning my eyes blur and I am pulled into another vision.

The house looks almost the same, but lined with candles—placed with purpose. In the front greeting room, more candles are visible, and I can see them lined up on the floor with the door wide open, flickering as if they have been waiting for my attention. The house seems simpler, more rustic. An era from long ago.

I creep towards the door, afraid of what I will find inside the room. My heart is pounding through my ears, so it is all I hear. Whatever time I'm in, there is another door in the back of the room that links out to the outside, because I can see the storm still raging behind the window. A crying sky setting the scene the way only nature knows how.

I turn to look to my right and realize this is not the estate anymore, but some place that resembles more of a castle. With stone walls and thick wooden doors. A large, engraved plaque taking up most of the wall hangs above where I stand now. It greets me with intimidation, bearing the design of a red lion as I look up at its expansiveness. A medieval coat of arms.

I turn again to get a better view of the room, something swinging in the distance. My eyes focus on the object as a heavy, oppressive feeling crushes down upon me. I freeze in place.

A paralyzing fear stops my muscles from working. The screen doors in the house open and slam shut repeatedly just as a soft scratching sound—like nails moving back and forth against a chalkboard—makes my stomach turn.

A woman with pale skin hangs from the banister in a white nightgown. The rope bound tightly around her neck creaks like a warning. The tips of her bare toes skim the floor, creating a sound I will never forget. My eyes open wide as I'm frozen by the weight of what I am seeing. This isn't just a stranger I'm looking at. It is me.

Startled by this unexpected sight, I rush out of the room and am instantly taken back to the present day. The rain is still pounding down outside, and now, so is my heart as I make my own rain in the form of cascading tears down my cheeks. I attempt to settle the rapid beating within, trying to convince myself that what I saw could have never taken place. After all, here I am in the flesh, alive and well.

I sit in place for God knows how long. The storm continues booming outside, and I know I must continue securing the windows. My legs tremble as I lock up the rest of the house. With no one to talk to, I feel just as mad as my uncle must have felt. I have been constantly shoved into the unknown since coming to this house. A portal of sorts that opened the moment I walked through its door.

I've heard of such things in stories growing up, *Alice in Wonderland* being one such book. However, whenever I would speak of it, my mother would always hush me and tell me not to fret over fantasy. But there is a fantasy to my visions that is encroaching on my reality, and it envelops me in a chaotic sense of familiarity I can deny no longer.

Alice had never felt as if she had been in Wonderland before, but with each vision, I feel closer and closer to where I have always belonged. My mind being my most powerful portal, taking me not actually to a place of fantasy, but perhaps to the realest, most concrete reality I have ever known. Even when parts of it feel like hell on earth.

———

The rest of the night does nothing for my nerves. The forest making itself known in every aspect of this house calms me a bit as I hold the warm painted teacup with branches along its side. Everything about the makings of this house feels like whoever created it wanted to bring the forest and all of its beauty inside. Maybe that is why I feel so at home in its presence.

Snuggling up to Carya, I crawl into bed but still can barely settle.

My best bet is to read—a sure way to clear my head after the night I just experienced. I bring the tattered green book closer, looking at the craftsmanship that surely must be over a hundred years old. Turning to the first page, hoping to dive into an ancient fantasy that doesn't resemble any of my horrid illusions.

The first chapter bears a small picture of hickory leaves and tells a tale belonging to the Druids. A story of ancient tree Beings within the roots that speaks of a time unknown to man. In this tale, a young tree sprite, created to provide power in the form of her own blood for a most insatiable tree Being, vanished before he could claim any control over her. Protected by her mother, she hides in the mortal world, in human form from the one who craves her most.

I turn the page, hoping to know more about this spellbinding folktale, but the next pages fall apart to powder against my fingertips. Most of the paper inside has been burned, making the words unreadable, and time making the pages unable to retain their dignity. I frown at the sad outcome of this book.

However, the endpapers bear some markings, their thickness holding up despite the rest of the pages of the book. A variety of tree species are drawn as if alluding to some sort of family tree or patriarchal hierarchy. They must belong to another Druid belief about the ancient tree Beings they believe ruled them.

Underneath each tree illustration holds a brief description. Under the oak, inked in gold embossing, reads *The Rooted Realm of Oak and Oath*. And there are others, all under their respective tree names. *The Rooted Realm of Pine and Pride. Hickory and Heart. Ash and Action. Cypress and Charisma. Cherry and Choice.*

I scan the page looking for the one to bring me the comfort I need most as I sit in this bed with my cozy feline. None of this is real, but it might still fill the missing piece in my heart. So, I skim along the tree-filled endpapers with my unpolished pointer finger, hoping what I find will give me some reassurance. And it does. Under a beautifully sketched willow reads, in loopy cursive, *The Rooted Realm of Willow and Worth*.

My lids grow heavy as I continue to make out some pages that didn't fall to pieces upon my touch. The book bobbing against my face as I grasp at any type of rest. I know I drift off at times, sleep knocking, but my anxious mind not letting it in. Those moments of slumber riddled with dreams of tree roots, damp moss, a dirt-stained dress and soft earth under my nails.

Or, much as I hoped it wouldn't, my mind trails off to the vision of me hanging there amongst the candles. A girl lost to her internal anguish. Apart from the shock of what I was seeing, it felt as if I belonged there in that vision. Like I had been there before.

My visions inhabit me, crawling into the synapses within my mind, creating a distant perception of a parallel life I had truly lived in. Those are the ones that seem to have picked up since coming to this estate. A life lived once, where there was just as much warmth and passion as pain and destruction, all stemming from this house and something else. Or perhaps *someone* else.

10

RECORD PLAYER

RACINE 1978

Rain taps the windows steadily with no sign of stopping anytime soon. The house has no television or radio, so I have to base my knowledge of the incoming weather on a gut feeling. A confusing instinct that hasn't been hitting its mark lately.

I still have a few boxes to sort through, but my attention wants to move toward the library. The dark green velvet plush chairs inside, inviting me to grab a book and sit. I would love to find another book like the one about the trees, but I'm afraid to look for any more that old in case they have fared as well as the other.

Putting my need for literary escapism aside, I pour myself into another box, hoping for a distraction. I have ultimately decided not to take what is in the boxes to a resale shop. The more I gazed upon pieces like the pearl necklace with the green studded pendant or the ornate silver mirror compact inlaid with moon crested abalone detail, the more my heart would ache at the thought of parting with them. Everything in them holds a sort of weird, unlocked recollection for me.

Perhaps I am grasping at a memory of an uncle I didn't know and wanted to—at least that is the excuse I tell myself. But it's more than that. To be honest, I've been picking up on odd past moments the more time I spend with some of these items. My visions can do that, blur the line of my own memories and someone else's altogether. It has happened since I was a kid. Many of the items at the shop had the same entrancing effect.

Down to the last box, I'm happily greeted by the familiar clear rectangular lid on a wooden turntable, the gold needle jumping into my line of sight as an ecstatic proclamation of acknowledgment. It looks a little worse for wear, the round black mat showing signs of heavy use, but I think it may still work. Of all the items I have found in the boxes, this is one I actually feel I can get the most use out of. And with my very unsubtle procrastination yelling obnoxiously in my ear, I figure there is no better time than the present.

I pull it out and blow off the thin layer of dust, watching it swirl into the air in a scattering of sparkles above me. My biggest regret is not bringing any records with me as I look down at the empty player with a frown. If my mind hadn't been such a directionless mess upon leaving, maybe I would have planned out my stay a little better. My hands rummage through drawers and move books, looking for a hidden spot where my uncle might have stored some. But, no luck. I give up with a sigh, and drop into the green velvet chair beside the bar.

That's when the idea hits me. Ry. Perhaps the mysterious man holds the key to my current dilemma. Or maybe I just want an excuse to see him again. I walk to the kitchen and dial the number on his business card that still sits on the dark cream marble counter. After a couple of rings, I am met with the gravelly hello I hadn't realized I was pining for until he spoke.

"Hey Ry," I start, "it's Jade..."

"I know," he replies curtly. I see he is still winning in the greetings department.

"OK...well, I found a record player here, but no records. I was wondering if you might help a girl out? Do you own any?" I can almost feel his grin behind the phone. Thank God. I was beginning to think this call had been a mistake, given the way his nonexistent banter hinted heavily at his displeasure with my unexpected call.

"Be right over. Oh, and Jade? No tea this time, just the strong stuff." His voice is sure and wanting now. He blows hot and cold, but when he is hot, I can feel it like a bolt of electricity through my system. I hang up, my stomach doing tiny flips in the process.

Feeling the excitement of his return to the estate, I quickly make use of the bar where there is indeed the strong stuff. It is clear my uncle loved his libations, and I am more than grateful for that unhealthy vice of his. I look over his collection earnestly until I find one that suits my fancy.

A cherry rum liquor labeled Havana Club sits on the bar cart in an oddly shaped bottle, begging to be tasted. It should know better than to beg, because I need little convincing. I reach to fill a small whisky glass that sits beside it and with one swig I am ready for a refill as I wait for my guest.

Within half an hour, Ry is at the front door with a handful of records. I snatch them out of his with excitement. The single eyebrow quirked at me, speaking volumes. I am beyond intrigued to know more about Ry, and nothing gives more insight into someone than the music they choose to fill their head with.

I look at the records in my hands. There are only about six, but I am shocked by what I'm holding. Ry's records and the ones I left back in Detroit are essentially the same. Surprise eats up my words. The fact that this man listens to the same music makes me wonder if my attraction to him could be more than just surface level.

I put one on without thinking. *Dancing in the Moonlight* by King Harvest fills the room. Honestly, it seems fitting for this house with its entrancing, dark mood that has been pulsating throughout since the day after I arrived.

The cherry liquor hits fast, warming my limbs. I feel bold and sway to the music as I pour him a glass. The tune float through the room, adding the last needed touch of comfort. Ease reverberates through me like the soft evening sound of the peeper frogs I hear reaching my bedroom window at night from the swamp below.

I turn around to hand Ry his drink, but his eyes are already on me. My cheeks redden, and my stomach dips. Will it always feel this way? I try to regroup as I head in his direction, his drink and my embarrassment to tag along.

"Believe it or not, we have similar music tastes." I say dryly, handing him his drink. Our fingers brush, sending my nerve synapses into overdrive.

These types of moments, touches, reactions or whatever they are, are hard to ignore. Ry is good at hiding his, but I see the small things. The crease on his forehead when we accidentally touch. The way his eyes dip down as if not to be seen when we stare a little too long.

"I believe it." He says, looking me square in the eye. "And to make this record roulette a little more interesting, I'll pick the next one."

I nod. His intensity pushes me into silence as our eyes link. His, the color of sea-foam, and mine, a purple grey. The way he looks through me is unnerving, like he can see me for more than just what he's known of me in these few short meetings. It's disarming and, admittedly, quite addictive.

"So, Ry Heart, would you call Racine your favorite place?" I ask partly because I'm curious, but also to break the silence that hangs heavy in the space between us.

"Uh, well, there have been many places I find appealing." He seems uncomfortable with my question, fidgeting with the hem of his shirt. His unease seems a bit out of character. Everything I've seen from him is sure, even if disagreeable. But he soon continues, "I move around quite a bit. But yes, I always come back. This town has always felt like a home base. Lots of memories here, you could say."

"Good ones, I imagine," I ask and tuck a strand of hair behind my ear. An anxious habit I have when I don't quite know what to say.

Ry looks up at me in that moment, like he is seeing me for the first time. He brings his hand up, pausing near my face as if questioning his next move, but drops it back down as he answers my question.

"Good and bad. There are always both wherever I am, unfortunately." His eyes grow heavy with remorse. "But more good than bad here, I guess. Maybe that is why I keep coming back," he says as he swirls his drink around in his tumbler. "OK, my turn." He stands, and I can't help being surprised by the openness of his answer.

Right Down the Line by Gary Rafferty sounds off the player. This song has always been one of my favorites, but listening to it in this room with him hits differently. These are his records, full of songs that have called to my heart since the time I first heard them.

He surprises me, and I am even more surprised when he holds his hand out to me. I take it, feeling the roughness of his in contrast to the softness of mine. My heart and body leading the way. He inches closer to me, wrapping his hand around my waist and resting it on my lower back. His seeking eyes feeding the fire between us, and I want nothing more but to burn in them. Be devoured by this moment.

I snake my arms around his neck and watch his face, inspecting for any hint of aversion. But the energy I am experiencing feels mutual. Even more so when I brush the back of his hairline with my thumb and he responds with the clench of his jaw.

"My dear, I find you quite dangerous to my wellbeing." He looks down at my neck, his words all but a whisper in my ear.

"How so?" I ask boldly, although I can't tell if it is the alcohol or the vibration humming around us that gives me my courage. The question gets lodged in my throat as I try to swallow and wait for his response.

"Dangerous, because I feel you unrooting parts of myself that should remain buried," he swallows, his throat bobbing with the action. He then utters the last bit close to my ear, "for your sake." I feel the words tickle my neck.

"Do you not think I will like those parts of you?" I ask, curious as

I am now holding on to his bicep. I squeeze slightly as he tightens his arm around my waist, and brings me closer still. I'm pressed to him, flush with his scent—earthy and safe.

I bring my head back to look into his eyes. They hold so much familiarity, feeling so thoroughly absorbed in them that his next comment leaves only a slight shock.

"Oh, I think you would love those parts of me, so much so that it might destroy us." He looks at me, his gaze dark and unwavering.

"I don't understand." I inquire, looking at him intently for the answer, while thinking his comment strange. But also deep down, I know what he is referring to. I can easily see myself coming apart for this man.

"No, you don't, little succulent, and that's the dangerous part." He says as he puts his lips to my hair and inhales. "I think it's time for me to head home." He pulls away, leaving too much space between us. "I'll leave the records. Call me when you are up in the morning, and I'll show you around Racine if you'd like. The bridge is something you'll want to see in person...Goodnight, Jade."

He kisses my hand in farewell, and just like that is out the door. Leaving me breathless, wound up, and so completely in need of more.

11

WILLOW WARNING
RACINE 1978

After Ry leaves, his absence is felt immediately. An open void. When he was here, my body pulsed with a recognition I couldn't unwrap in my mind. It seemed buried deep within, much like tree roots knotted beneath old earth. No matter how hard I try to pry this silent sense of knowing out, it remains stuck. The roots too deep and comfortable in their position to release any bit of information.

I lock up the house and head to the kitchen for a glass of water. A snag in my periphery that I can't ignore is the basement door, because it somehow has become cracked open yet again. The lock must be faulty, and I curse my luck at that.

I run over to it, faster because my comfy socks let me slide across the hardwood floor, slamming it shut. Long, thin, dried purple petals float up with the gust of air. The strong musty smell that blasts out from behind it floods my nostrils. It isn't a good or bad smell, but it makes me uneasy. Dark, damp, earthy, and eerie like an old warren. One that used to be home to a rabbit family, but now only their bones remain beside a very full fox.

I turn and rest my head against the door. For a minute, I am swayed to open it and head into its depths. My good sense proves too strong, and I talk myself out of it. How a basement even remains intact in this part of Louisiana baffles me.

I look down at the floor. One lone feather sits softly at my feet. But this feather isn't from one of the many luxurious down pillows on the estate. This feather stands out. It doesn't belong inside. It belongs to a bird I've seen soar through the property skies. A hawk.

———

Once upstairs, I throw on my nightshirt, and glance out the window toward the swamp. It is a half-moon tonight, and looking out at its reflection on the watery glass is a scene of magic. The moon dusts the bayou with a shimmer, as if fireflies dance beneath its surface. It is breathtaking, and I still cannot believe that all this is mine.

I think of Detroit, the city I've claimed as my own all these years, its hold on me slipping as if it were never really my home at all. The longer I stay down here, the harder time I have imagining going back. The willow outside seems to respond to my thoughts by sweeping its branches along the water's edge, as if it has some say in the way I'm feeling about this place.

I fall under the covers easily. Today was unexpected, but I found I wanted whatever Ry was feeding me while we danced to the song that felt like our own. It would have taken everything I am not to have kissed him if that was what he wanted, and it seemed, for a moment, he may have. I close my eyes, and for a brief time imagine that kiss happening. And that feeling of comfort comes again, because it feels as if our lips are calling out to meet each other after being apart for so long.

My dreams flow fluidly that night. Dreams of Ry morph to me standing next to the old hickory from my youth. I feel at home, but my mother is there, and then her hugs wrap around me with the grace of willow branches. Each dream is like the next, but more vivid.

Then something shifts, and gone is the calm as panic stirs up within my mother's voice.

She is pulling me away from the old hickory. Terror in her eyes and words faint, but growing. By the last one, I can finally hear a whisper that expands to a shrill as it continues building intensity. My mother's voice, whose words I will never forget.

There is no heart in hickory. There is no heart in hickory. There is no heart in hickory. There is no heart. He has NO HEART. RUN.

I wake up, my own heart racing with the odd sense that my mother's words hold a hidden truth. And I cannot think of anything but the man with Heart as his last name.

12

THE PROPERTY
RACINE 1978

After a week of torrential rain here and the ongoing process of going through the house, I still haven't ventured to the basement or out to explore the property. The rain is the cause of the latter, but it is anxiety that keeps me from opening the basement door again.

Fortunately, today the rain finally clears, as do the cobwebs of disillusion that it may never stop. As I step outside, the warm and still damp air fills my lungs. I welcome the sun's heat wafting the smell of waking florals. I find myself wearing a relaxed smile as I take a step down towards the wraparound porch.

Visions still plague me since coming here. Growing more and more constant since finding the ring and the box it belongs in. The ring sits up in my room on the desk overlooking the willow near the pond. A part of me wants to slide it on my finger to see if it fits. Another part of me knows it will. But at least with the weather change, I can feel less consumed by its looming presence and more devoted to exploring this beautiful land.

I planned a meeting with Ry to discuss how to allocate my finances. My goal being to keep this house, while also maintaining my shop. Even though the topic of discussion is rather boring to me, I am giddy to see him again.

Yesterday was a turning point in the realization of how strong my attraction is to him. He is dark, serious, but magnetic all the same. He will meet me here within the hour, leaving me a good amount of time to get to know the layout of the property.

The moment my feet step off the last step, I know exactly the direction I am heading. The walk there is maybe five or so minutes even though I can already see it from here, standing tall and superior. And the excitement it invokes when I see it there is not one I've felt in a while. Not that inheriting a house isn't exciting, but I have a kinship toward trees, so this part of the inheritance feels more like second nature. And one type of tree in particular has been calling to me ever since I fully took it in from out the attic window.

I take a deep breath of warm, rich air that still smells of the wet earth soaking up the rain. A smell that is wholly unique to the bayou here. I curl my hand above my eyebrows, blocking the sun as I look up, my smile extending to my heart.

There in front of me is the largest hickory tree I have ever seen in my life, sitting deep on top of a small hill. Its roots have a mind of their own as they dip high and low, above and below the ground that the tree birthed from. The smallest purple thistle plant grows underneath, seeming almost out of place amongst its knotted roots.

I have never seen anything so magnificent. And it doesn't take long for the magnificence and wonder of it to seep slowly into me, fixing itself to the depths of my bones. But just as my bones soak in the beauty of that feeling, there is another feeling fighting to replace it. A hollow sadness curls its way into my chest. I felt this in my shop just weeks ago, and here it sits again at the pit of my stomach.

I collapse to the ground as tears fall without warning down my cheeks. This sadness shouldn't belong to me, but it covers me like a weighted blanket closing down on my chest. I wipe my eyes, and try to take a few steps closer to the tree. But with every step, the heartache grows stronger.

My hand goes to my chest trying to pull out the anguish within. I just want to reach out and touch one of the branches or sit within the root-formed circle that seems just for me. But this unknown heart hurt is too much to bear, and I cannot be here any longer, even if some deeper force inside my soul begs me to stay.

I turn away regretfully, needing relief from the foreign emotions working through me. The farther I get from the tree, the less my heart aches. It's a strange occurrence I've never experienced before. How can something pull me in so strongly only to repel my whole being the moment I get close? It was heartbreak in its raw form, and I had only felt it once before.

What I knew of love, I learned from my mother. I knew what loss was because of her, too. And the feeling I just felt at this tree is so similar to the feeling my heart went through when she passed. An unbearable ache in my chest that I reckon could crack my whole body in half. But there was an angry twist to this ache, making it different somehow. Perhaps, a different form of love being broken.

Not far off from the hickory is a large oak. Standing on its own and seeming to take up more land than is necessary. It sits perched, leaning to one side, as if it can't believe it is only just now being noticed. As I walk towards it, I see a massive limb has fallen on one side. It looks fresh, making me think back to the loud crash I heard a few days earlier when the storm raged its hardest. It must have been this poor oak making itself known as part of it smashed to the ground from the strike.

I've always loved oaks. They carry a certain truth about them that speaks out through their branches. The way they twist and turn and reach out to keep searching for what is beyond them. And the darkness that comes with all that truth lingers on this oak in the deep crevices of its bark. I think of the word written underneath its illustration in that beautiful tattered book. *Oath.* How very fitting.

I pass the fallen limb and notice in its destruction it has also snapped a branch off the neighboring tree. When one falls from grace in such a dramatic manner, they're bound to take down a few others along the way. I guess the same goes for trees.

Turning toward the house, I walk to the small pond in the back, where the willow stands in all her nurturing glory. Already I feel lighter making my way to the tree that my mother always loved. I float past tall and straight pines and curvy, ropey cypress trees. I all but run toward the welcoming willow, letting the dangling curtain-like leaves brush upon my skin.

As a kid, I would swing from willow branches, having so much trust that they would never let me fall. I sit down under its enormous trunk, closing my eyes and staying still beneath the tree facing toward the sun. The soft rays bleed a soothing warmth into my essence. Accepted is how I feel here. Not just at this tree, but at the house, at this property. Well, now apart from the hickory.

I can only imagine how I will take to the town. Will I have the same silent knowing of a life that belonged to me there? My thoughts turn toward the jade ring. A broken but whole artistry about it. Perhaps it will not even fit—that is, if I ever find the nerve to try it on. And where is the ring marked Opal? And why are both in such a unique box?

I try to settle my mind and relax a bit into the trunk of the tree. Words are whispered in the breeze. Faint and soft like a mourning dove's gentle coo. *A choice was made, so you could live.* And then later the whisper changes to a louder hum as if someone were right in my ear. *Listen, my love. He is here. Guard your heart, for he does not possess one, and he will take yours at all costs.*

13
TOWN

RACINE 1978

A car rumbling down the drive is the first thing I hear after a long silence. I must have drifted off under the comfort of the old willow. Ry's vehicle comes into focus down the driveway. He probably can't see me from here, leaving me no choice but to rise and head in his direction.

A knot forms in my stomach, of nerves and worry, but as I get farther from the willow and closer to the car, it dissipates. My connection to the trees has never felt more prominent than it does here. Only here though, I find they meld together, and I can't tell which feelings actually belong to me—and which do not. It is a disconcerting feeling, and perhaps my uncle felt something similar.

Ry is out of the car now. The closer I get, the worry that wrapped itself around my spine turns into increasing thrill. I greet him with a mischievous smile as he puts one arm on the top of the door.

One should not look the way he does. His muscles tense along his arms as he looks me over, a glint of a sparkle in his eye that I don't fail to notice. If he is anything like me, yesterday's almost events are replaying in his head.

"Hi...I was just out walking the property. I can see why my uncle never left. These trees...they hold a sort of...magic." I pause after I say these words because a small truth stirs in my heart. Magic is definitely what I feel here. "The storm did a bit of damage, though. Nothing too serious." Ry tenses at the last statement.

"Which trees were damaged?" He asks in an anxious, rushed tone.

"A large oak sadly. It took part of a cherry limb with it," I answer, wondering why he seems so worked up. A flash of irritation rolling through his eyes, which he closes briefly, saying his next words as calmly as he can.

"I will be happy to check them out later." He pauses, seeming to gain more composure before he adds, "Would you like to get lunch in town? I know a place."

I nod, looking forward to seeing a bit of the town. Lollie and Ash will be here before I know it, and Lollie will want me to scope out any dives. She is always the life of the party. As for me, I hope to find some antique shops. The history is this area is vast in richness, and I want to know all there is to be known.

But, to be honest, at this moment I am more intrigued with the tall brooding man that I'm about to get in the car with. We drive down the dirt road in silence, looking over at him periodically. Knowing what I feel seems to hum around the small space of this car, so he must feel it, too.

From this view, I get a good look at his profile. His eyebrows are thick and furrowed as if in deep thought. His lashes are longer than mine, with a straight nose. And oh, his lips. His bottom one full and I wonder what it might feel like on mine. His attention turns toward me as my eyes make their way up to his. Once I see I've been caught, I glance away.

"Don't turn your head. I find I enjoy your eyes on me." He says with a voice dripping with cocky confidence. I am so taken aback by his comment that I can only stare at him. Lost in the sea of his beauty and the storm brewing in his eyes that mimics the one forming in my chest, growing in waves, moving lower and lower within me.

"I'm sorry, I didn't mean to stare. I just got caught in thought," I stutter. A poor excuse, I know.

"Don't ever apologize for admiring. I do the same to you," he replies, and I'm yet again intrigued with his level of confidence.

A hint of a smirk graces those plump, kissable lips. *Shit.* My thoughts may betray me, but at least I can hold them together on my tongue. A tongue that wonders how his would taste against mine. And with that thought, I know I am supremely fucked. I blush all the way into town.

We eventually make it to our destination, and I focus on looking out the window hoping to get my mind clear of all current thoughts about the man next to me. The beauty of these historic houses does the trick.

Gracing the streets are tall, ethereal buildings. Two-story townhouses with pillars built in front that hold together two levels of porches. Some houses have a garden conjoined to them, separated by cast-iron railings; some are well kept, and others seem to be a mass of rose brambles. Brick stones make up the road, making the drive seem from a simpler era. I think one I would have liked very much.

We drift down the street and park next to one house that has a sign hanging out front. It reads, *The Spanish Moss* in bold dark pink letters against a white background. The sign looks fairly new, but the building itself looks as if it's seen centuries pass through its brick foundation.

"Well, here we are. This place has been around for years. Changed names and owners a handful of times," he says. He turns off the ignition. "As of right now, it's back to its original owner's great-great-grandson. Either way, I have a feeling you'll like the food." Ry seems so sure of his last comment.

"And how do you know what I'll like?" I retort, giving him a sideways glance with a bit of a jest.

He just directs an overly smug grin my way, his silence speaking volumes. Half an hour later, I'm shoving the best veggie omelet greedily in my mouth. Not realizing I was so badly in need of a good homemade meal. And wow, it is good. Ry sits across from me, sipping his coffee with eyes that read of his satisfaction of being right.

We have a pleasant talk about finances while we eat. One which mainly involves Ry telling me things, while I scarf down all the food placed in front of me. He presents the idea of my homesteading the estate so that taxes are more manageable.

"I think the details of your shop will come in time. Right now, you should focus on the present—on the house," Ry explains. I can't help but agree. This place has set its voodoo on me. I'm all in.

"So, you were right. This food is amazing," I finally cave, changing the subject and I admit defeat, putting the napkin on the empty plate before me.

"Ah, yes, I usually am, Jade," he says, his sureness shining through, "and it helps to know the owners. Would you like to meet them...Oh, well, never-mind, here they come."

Ry stands, and I can't help but notice how truly tall he is. He towers over the couple arriving to welcome us at our table. I quickly stand as well.

The two that greet me have beautiful moon-shaped eyes that speak of all the kindness they keep within. Here I was expecting a young couple, but these two are well into their sixties, and look at us as if we are the rare hidden gems in the room.

"Jade, let me introduce you to Walt and Cattie. These two are very dear old friends," Ry voices. I take their hands in greeting and am flooded with warmth and sincerity.

"Jade, it is so nice to see you. I imagine you are the one who has taken residence over The Rooted Realm Estate?" Cattie says. I look to Ry, surprise clearly on my face that they would know anything about me, but his face is indifferent. Cattie continues,"Hopefully, it is everything you've dreamt it would be. We used to visit that place long ago. We've always wondered if it fell apart over the years. Do tell, how has it held up?"

"Actually, for how old and massive it is, I would say it has held up really well. It seems taken care of, especially the property. And yes, I find I'm growing quite fond of it." I say, glancing over at Ry. But I have more questions on my mind to ask, so I continue, "You must have known my uncle if you say you've been there before?"

"Oh yes, we knew him well when he was younger. He would hold the most extravagant parties. Your uncle made sure we always had a good time, that is for sure." Cattie giggles as if lost in the wonderful memories of those parties.

Walt doesn't say much, but his stare does. A host to curiosity and something else I can't quite put my finger on.

"I think that is enough talk about Rowan's parties," Ry says, an edge cutting through in his tone. Why he doesn't want to talk about my uncle, I don't know, but the sweet restaurant owners change the subject quickly.

There isn't much talk after, but what little there is comes easy until we say our goodbyes. I promise to visit again. How can I not? I leave feeling lighter even though I ate my weight in food, and I am so pleased to have some form of knowledge of my uncle and the magic that the estate used to hold.

I'm deep in thought about the information I just learned when I feel a hand on the small of my back and a slight shock. It is Ry's, and the shock sends a current up my spine that produces a small gasp from my lips.

Ry acts as if nothing happened, of course. He looks me in the eye as we walk out the doors and points to a park across the way. It seems he has reverted to cold Ry since our conversation with *The Spanish Moss* owners.

"In a time before you and me, this park was the start of this town." His voice serious, but thawing. "There's a town myth that says it holds the memories of all that has happened here because of the river that runs through it." He still holds out his arm, making sure I see where it is directed before he continues. "It's the same river that connects all the way back to your very own Rooted Realm Estate," he says, his impromptu history lesson warming him some.

I look at the park, seeing a mass of old, gigantic oaks and hickories full of wispy Spanish moss. A beautiful stone bridge connects one land to the next, with a river down the middle. It is an eerily beautiful sight, and I take it in wholly, feeling I have been here before.

I walk to the bridge in hopes of going over it. The stones seem worn, but sturdy. I can only imagine what stories they hold in the quiet of their time here.

It is within seconds of taking one step on the bridge that I see a young woman with hair the color of mine, and a man I can't make out. Words are being hurled between them in argument. She is similar to the woman I saw on that stormy night, but different, too. She is crying and pushing him back, while he pulls at his hair in frustration.

In a flurry of motion, she stands unsteadily on the bridge, pulling out a knife. She moves the blade to each of her wrists, pushing down with force. Blood oozes out from the deep slicing of her veins. And with a splash, she jumps in. Just like that. The beautiful flowing river turning the deepest shade of red.

I suck in a deep breath and move my foot back off the bridge. The two are gone, as if it were all in my mind, because they were. Another vision I must tuck away, holding too much weight within me.

I turn and stare at the two hands that grasp tight to my shoulders. They are Ry's, and he looks furious, heartbroken even.

"Are you alright?" He asks visibly shaken, as if he could know what I just saw.

"I don't know...I mean, yes, sorry. I was just in my mind for a minute," I stammer. I can tell he doesn't believe me.

"Here, let's get you back home." Caring Ry makes a debut. He then adds, as if trying to ease the tension, "I'd like to check out those trees you said were damaged in the storm."

We both move along as if nothing transpired at all. In fact, maybe he couldn't tell anything was going through my mind in that moment on the bridge. The beauty of my visions being that I now know how to act *mostly* normal after I come back to the present. I push them back and do my best to retain my repose, hoping there will be no other surprise mind warps.

On the way back to the car, we pass a row of bars that scream Lollie's name. Ry says they are all usually pretty busy at night with locals but also the occasional tourists. The way he says it is as if I should be warned or turned off even. In truth, I'm a bit intrigued to see the nightlife of this small Louisiana town.

Looking at the city behind us, we drive away and head back to the estate. For the first time, I think back to Ry's comment about getting back home, and I think yes, this could quite actually be my home. Although I could do without all the haunting visions that seem to plague me here.

It takes about a twenty-five minute drive from town back to the estate, and the sun is making its way down to the other side of the horizon. Night is close, but neither of us is ready for our time together to come to a close.

Ry and I get out of the car. My promise of showing him the cracked oak tree I refuse to break. Our way of continuing to grace one another with curious looks that speak more words than our actual words do tonight.

As we walk, another buzz of energy floats among us. I swear he must feel it, too. He keeps stealing glances at me in my white mid-length sundress. I can feel his eyes on my face, then my neck. I feel them move lower to my chest, and I blush even though I am not looking at him.

His eyes make their mark known across my skin. Fire heats every spot they land on. I finally look at him, and my skin scorches to a crisp. And when I think he will look the other way, his presence darkens.

"As you can tell, I like my eyes on you, too." He smirks down at me.

My body instantly heats with excitement at those words. Not sure I heard him correctly, I pick up my pace and walk ahead. He quickens as well. A cat-and-mouse game with his eyes, hunting me down with their ferocity.

When we finally make it to the oak, I look up at him. Ry's eyes burn, but not in the way I am hoping. Anger floods out. His mood has changed again. Suddenly, he is quite different from the walk here.

"Is everything good?" I ask him, my eyebrows drawn in.

"Yes, it's just as I thought, is all," he growls, looking to the split oak tree. "I'll get these branches taken care of tomorrow."

He seems so disgruntled about the broken limbs that a short laugh leaves my mouth. The man who wears a thousand faces in a day. One minute he acts as if he has a vendetta against the world, and the next? The next minute he acts as if he wants to eat me alive.

My last comment seeming to have broken him from a spell. The surrounding atmosphere relaxes, and he closes the space between us.

"Please be careful around here. These trees are more dangerous than they look," he says, serious as hell, and I can't help but giggle again at that comment. "And stop with the giggles, please. They're distracting. Everything about you is distracting." His eyes burn again, but it is with something else. Desire? I push his last comment aside.

"How can trees be dangerous? I've never been hurt by a tree, Ry." He clenches his jaw like he wants to say something, but looks past me. It is then that I feel the pull of the hickory.

Maybe together, with him, the sadness within that tree wouldn't have such a grasp on me. I grab Ry's hand, and his eyes widen in surprise. Spinning on my heels, I pull him in my direction, making our way toward the tree that gave me so many emotions this morning.

"I want to show you something," I whisper behind me. It comes out breathy and full of the same things I saw in his eyes just a minute ago.

It takes five minutes to make our way to the tree, and in the meantime, the moon makes its way up to the center of the sky. I want to see if I feel the same things I did earlier, with Ry giving me added security.

I stop in front of the tree, but those feelings of sadness and heartache are gone. I take a step to get closer. The soft night breeze blows my dark copper curls against my face. I go to move them away from my eyes, but a hand is already there doing it for me.

I slowly look up to meet his candy-hued eyes, and I notice they are darker now. They are a color of the deepest sea green. A darker jade than my name can claim.

At that thought, I step closer to him so that each breath lingers against his chest. His hands wrap around my waist, securing me to him. Want grows deep, building to a crescendo I hope to make it to.

We stand there, caught in the invisible dance before something happens. How did we get here? When did we make the switch from new acquaintances to this—whatever *this* is? It doesn't feel as if we were just meeting for the first time. It feels fated.

The breeze comes again, and certain parts of my body respond to the unusual blast of cool air. He must feel it as I notice a pulse from below. We stand like that, both wanting but not moving.

I swear the earth rumbles below us as if the roots of the tree are stirring to life upon the notion of our proximity. I move up on my toes as he moves down to meet my face. His eyes dilate, moving his lips down lower to make this real.

And then it is all feathers and wings between us, followed by an obnoxious caw. Shocked by the commotion, we jump apart. The bird flies by again and toward the oak.

We both look at each other. He looks angry and agitated. I feel wound up, still hoping for a release I didn't get. Twisting my hands, I let out a breath. I can't believe what we were about to do, and under the hickory it felt so natural, welcoming even. A story that was destined, but ripped apart before it could be completed.

Somehow, we ease back into the reality of the situation. He turns and starts walking back toward the house.

"We should go," he says gruffly, his feet already moving toward the house. Annoyed at his change in attitude, I start after him.

"Are you serious?" I question. How is he going to act like what just happened didn't?

"Yep. No good can come out here. Not when they are watching." He says still charging ahead toward the house. I huff a noise of disbelief. *Who* is watching?

I lift the skirt of my dress and bunch it in my hands so I can move forward briskly. With my chin high, so as to make sure he notices, I march toward the house, pushing past him in irritation.

We pass the old oak, and I feel the eyes of the crow as we rush by, as if pleased with itself for causing such a disruption. Making my way to where Ry's car sits, I keep walking past it. Anger and pride running like thick syrup through my veins.

"You can see your way out." My voice holding a bitter note of disgust.

The echo of the car door and the headlights hit harshly at my back. A sure highlight of my current 'don't give a shit' state of mind. I don't dare look behind me, afraid my face will give away what I'm really feeling. I'm embarrassed I let myself feel anything, only for him to toss it aside like nothing.

Ry's car is now well down the drive as I shut the front door behind me, and lock it. I slide down the back of it, a deep frown woven into my face and my heart. That was not how I saw the night going. Not in the least. But, it's safe to say that perhaps Ry and I will be doing business strictly by the phone from now on.

Carya walks between my outstretched legs and then nudges my hand. She has always been my creature of comfort, knowing when I need her to stir my splintered heart back to a content rhythm.

For a minute, I had let my ideas of romantic idealism get away from me. It was easy to do when that man looked the way he did at me, but it stirred the hopeless romantic in me a little too much. It will not happen again, even if deep down I hope it will.

A hint of the heartbreak I felt before at the hickory nudges its way through. A single tear falls down my cheek, my eyes closing at its appearance. Look at me, letting a man I've known not even a month affect me this way. Silly girl, you should know better.

Making my way up the stairs to the bed, I strip off my dress and throw on one of my old band t-shirts, half-heartedly wash my face, brush my teeth and all but fall into bed. I never want to be reminded of tonight, and I don't care if I ever see Ry again.

With that lie, I close my eyes and let my body do its best to numb my mind to sleep.

FLASHBACK
DACIA 140 AD * PRESENT DAY ROMANIA

The only way to get water for our small farm was a half-mile walk down a winding dirt road. A well lay on the edge of woods that I had yet to venture in, mostly out of fear. Stories circled the woods by the well, and at nineteen, I'd learned to heed their warning. However scared I was when I retrieved water, I was also mesmerized.

Feeling eyes on me that could not possibly be there. The townspeople would talk of demons within those woods. A warning if you made your way deep within, you did not come back the same. That is, if you came back at all.

Seeing the well within sight, I pick up my steps. My daily chore of retrieving water has become one I both anticipate and dread. The ground crunches beneath my feet, littered with the recent cuttings of dried millet stalks.

I lower one large water pail into the well, listening to hear the familiar splash of water as the pail hits its now rippling surface. I drag it up, keeping my eyes on the tree line ahead, feeling my work a show for whoever roams within. The pines, oaks and hickory hum their siren song to me in the form of leaves rustling in the breeze.

Out of the corner of my eye, I see movement. My vision is always playing tricks on me at this time of night. There are deer that live within these woods, so I account it being one of them trying to evade my notice.

I turn to leave with two buckets full of water, but a hawk sits in the middle of my trail. It stands still and regal, blocking my path. Its eyes reflecting the lowering sun, a perspective I would hope to see in another life. Eyes that speak of something else, too. A hidden secret that it wants to tell.

Before it seems it may speak, it flies off with something dropping from its talons and landing amongst the hardened stalks at my feet. I scoop it up, seeing that it is not some rotten piece of dead carrion like one would expect, but a ring made of a dark golden metal. Metal leaves and opaque green stones are laid within as I examine it inside the shallow dip of the palm of my hand.

Turning it against my fingers, I hear a whisper that directs me back to the tree line. I hold the ring in my fist, and walk closer to the forest, eyes searching beyond the wooden trunks. I could walk in. It would be so easy, and the curiosity flowing through me is nudging me further. The toes of my bare feet skim dangerously close to the edge where the first tree appears.

Deep within, I see larger wooden tree forms whispering words of encouragement in hopes I will come see what the forest holds. One large tree in particular tugs at my attention. I can almost feel the grip of its branches on my body as I go to take a step in.

The bell on the farm rings, meaning Mother has made supper. I startle, falling back on my heels, and turn back toward the path leading to my house. Saving my 'could be grave adventure' for another day.

My mother always has some instinctual feeling when I am about to do something I should not. I curse her sixth sense. It would be a cold day in hell when I can finally break the rules she has so firmly set in place.

I carry the water back, glimpsing behind me at the forest every few steps. Once out of sight, I exhale the nervousness that filled my lungs.

The first bucket I take to the pigs and goats, and the second I bring up to the house for our own personal use.

During supper, my mother looks at me skeptically. It is only us at the table. My aunt, who lives here too, retired early for the night, unhappy with my delayed return.

"What took so long?" She finally asks. I respond with a shrug and feed her some lie about getting distracted by the beauty of the sunset. It works since I am often awestruck with how nature can wholly consume one in its being, and my mother knows this about me.

She is fragile, and has become more so as time goes by. Sometimes I think it is because she worries about me too much, but I know it must be something more. An ailment that makes her pale and faint. One that gets worse as we live on this barren land.

I don't lie to be defiant, but to protect her. I'd hate to have her bedridden because of a risk I almost took. As I finish my supper, I think about this, toying pensively with the ring in the corner of the small pocket of my dress.

After I clean up the dishes, I scoop up a cup of leftover water, grab a clean rag and make my way up to my bedroom. Dipping the rag in the slightly cold water, I diligently wash off the stubborn dirt staining my skin, and shrug into my nightgown.

I keep the candle lit on my nightstand as I study the ring within my fingers. Turning it over and over to memorize every detail. It looks about my size, so without hesitating I slip it on my left hand. It slips easily onto my ring finger. A tingle starts, then swells into a rush of unwelcome knowing that floods through me.

Visions curse me. Visions of heavy wooden doors intertwined deep within tree roots, opening to a whole new world under this one. And of a woman with willow branches for hair holding me as a mother would. Of extravagant beds with messy sheets involving a shadow of a man with dark brown hair and markings resembling tree bark, who lurks beneath the earth.

14

THE WOOD

RACINE 1978

The next morning, I wake from my slumber to the sound of steady, rhythmic chopping outside. Glancing out the window, I see Ry is here splitting the wood he must have hauled off from the damaged oak. So much for never seeing him again.

It's not even eight in the morning, meaning he must have gotten here before seven. Another thing I can mark on our list of differences. I have never been a morning person, nor will I ever be.

A hawk sits quietly perched atop the white birdhouse that stands off on its own atop a tall pole—an obvious replica of the estate I stand in now. The hawk casting a shadow over the entirety of it.

I press a hand to my chest, my attention drawn back to the shirtless man working beneath my bedroom window. I can see the way the sun hits the sweat on his body, following along the slopes of his lean muscles as he swings the axe down on the wood. He swings again. The incessant chopping motion becoming wildly mesmerizing.

Admiring Ry's looks I've learned is alarmingly easy—but then I remember last night. Last night, when we almost kissed until one damn bird turned the entire night sour, including his attitude. He couldn't get away from me fast enough then, so what the hell is he doing here now? My hope was I wouldn't see him again, at least not this soon.

I pull on some sweats that lay crumbled on the wooden chest at the end of the bed and go down to make some coffee. Passing the door to the basement, I notice it is again slightly ajar and I quickly slam it shut. I'm about as fed up with that door as I am with grumpy men showing up uninvited.

Heading to the kitchen, I can't decide if I want to face Ry or not. Last night was so awkward, and I know today may lead to even more awkwardness on my part. But I won't think too much about it. I refuse to let him ruin my mood on my own property.

I grab a coffee and a water and make my way out to face him the only way I know how. Forcefully, I hold them both out to him. Showing him yes, I'm still very upset. As far as I'm concerned, we never have to talk about last night again. He made it very clear that he wants nothing to do with me with the way he dashed off.

I imagine he is thinking the same thing about never seeing each other again when he takes the water out of my hands. I soon realize I am mistaken in my silly perception of his thoughts. He holds my gaze the whole time he drinks from the water glass, eyeing me as I were the next thing to quench his thirst. The sheer intimacy of the act making me melt under the hot morning sun.

"Uh, good morning," I finally fumble out, wrapping my arms around me as I am now realizing I forgot to put a bra on before leaving the house. "I did not expect you to be here."

"I told you I would take care of the oak, didn't I?" Ry says, like I shouldn't have expected anything less.

Well, if anything, I guess he is a man of his word. I can't help but roll my eyes, thinking he probably didn't catch it. My mistake. Within a second, he is towering over me, and I am met with an up-close and personal view of all his sweat-glistening skin with markings that mimic the scenery around us.

I watch as one drop of moisture travels from the middle of his sternum all the way down to the buckle of his belt and then slips under his jeans.

"I'd be careful what you do with those eyes, my dear. You can keep them on me all day. In fact, I prefer it. But the minute you roll them at me, I'll take that as permission to be rolling my tongue somewhere on you." Heat spreads through me at his words. Did he really just say that?

I look up into his eyes, and bite my lip thinking of where that place would be. His eyes speak on that challenge, because dear God he knows exactly what I am thinking. With my lip still fastened between my teeth, I decide to look directly at him. Courage finds me then and, against my better judgement, I roll them again.

In a heartbeat, he wraps his large fingers loosely around the side of my throat with one hand, guiding my body up against the hood of his red work truck. I watch as his head dips down, *finally* touching his lips to mine softly, then again with more pressure. I have been craving this since he chimed the bell on my shop door. I pray it doesn't stop.

I let out a breathy moan involuntarily, giving away my reaction to his lips. He looks at me with eyes that seem to have taken on pure darkness. They are not sea-foam green anymore. Now they are a dark, stormy sea full of need.

I know exactly what he is giving with those eyes, because mine speak of the same. I know I want this man. Even if just for one moment. And it is clear that moment is now.

His lips have moved to my neck, and he trails kisses down the center to between my breasts. Now I know what they feel like, and I only want more. Without lifting his head, he tugs my shirt down over my bare breasts as I lie there exposed.

My hair fans out around his red pickup truck, and I look up to see the hawk is no longer atop the birdhouse, hopefully flown away once seeing what was about to take place. His mouth finds one of my erect nipples, while his hand moves back up to my neck to hold me down against the sun-warmed, red metal against my back.

He flicks the bud of my nipple with his tongue, and I look down to see he is looking up right at me. His tongue forming circles against me. *My God.* His eyes hold mine as if agreeing with that last thought, though he has no way of knowing.

He tightens his hand around my neck just enough that I know he can feel my pulse throbbing. I let my head drop back again, unraveling as he lets his other hand skim the top of my panties. His fingertips dip beneath them and run along the lace trim.

Although we have only just met in the last few weeks, I feel I've been waiting so long for this. *Too* long. He takes his fingers out from under my panty line, and brushes the tips over the fabric of my sheer blush-colored panties, wetness soaking through. I gasp at his touch, wanting him to explore more.

"Mmmm, that's a good girl," he says as he feels how drenched I am. My entire body hums at his praise, and I think I hear the call of a hawk somewhere, begging it to keep its distance. This event being a non-spectator sport and all. The sound makes me wake up faintly to the realization that we are still outside.

"Wait," I panic. "We should go inside. What if someone comes down the driveway?"

With that comment, he fists one side of my panties up so the fabric is tight against my most sensitive area. The sheer friction of it making me squirm beneath him. He brings his other hand down to hold the other side of the panty up tight.

Slowly, he tugs each side in a rocking motion, making the damp fabric rub my clit, sending the most delicious sensations to my core. I can feel the pressure building, ebbing back and forth as he rocks back and forth. All the while, his stare is unmoving, daring me to tell him to stop.

"The fuck I care who sees us? It's just the trees out here—and they already know you belong to me." His words hit where they're meant to, any reserve between us dissolving immediately.

Ry slams his mouth into mine, pulling me up the hood of the car by the sides of my panties. I gasp under his lips as I hear one side rip from the force of that pull. Releasing my mouth, he pulls back to push the ripped panty to the side, leaving full access to my swollen pussy.

He looks down at it, then back to me, his eyes dilating and his breathing quickening. I know what he is thinking. *Please.* I nod my head, my eyes barely open with arousal.

In one decisive motion, he dips down and licks from the core of me and up. Finding the nub of my clit and sucking it into his mouth. He rolls his tongue around it, doing a ballet of moves I can't focus on, but I feel the results.

His fingers find their way inside me, pumping one, then two, in and out. Curling them just enough to hit a spot I didn't know could feel the way it does.

"Keep going," I think I say, although I can't be sure the words form.

Just as soon as I'm about to find my release, he pulls them out and smacks my center with his hand. A loud gasp of surprise fills the open air, falling only on Ry's ears. The act leaves me wanting more.

Looking at me with eyelids heavy with want, Ry steps back. Gazing at my naked body, there is only one thing he can do now, and I crave for him to do it.

He undoes his belt, then his zipper, pulling out his hard length. I take it all in, knowing I will feel every inch of him.

"Wait," I squeak. The enormity of what we are about to do seeps in—of what we have done already.

"Maybe this is too much…or too fast, I think?" He looks down at me while pumping himself; looking part animal, part God. The tattoos etched along his arms shimmer in the sun, seeming almost like magic.

"Do you not want this?" he asks with his eyebrows drawn into each other. He is serious now, as though some of his vulnerability has leaked through the walls he normally has up. He thinks I doubt our need for each other. How could I let him think that? There is nothing I want more. There is no one I want more.

"No, I definitely do," I say, and then again, "I want all of it."

With that answer, he relaxes and grabs me by the shirt, still bundled below my breasts, pulling me up into him. He wraps his arm around my waist, the other one landing on one side of my behind. Strong arms scoop me up, my legs having no choice but to wrap around his torso. As he slowly eases into me.

Our eyes lock. A connection fitted much like the timeless lock and key sets that sit on a shelf in Detroit. He stretches me so I can feel every bit of his thickness, and the feeling it sparks is pure fire. And if fire could make music, it would sing this exact tune coursing through our bodies right now.

With our faces mere inches apart, we find a rhythm of me bouncing back onto him and him into me. He is hitting a spot within me over and over. Arousal growing, taking me closer and closer to the edge. His stomach muscles tighten with each thrust, and his hand on my bottom digs in deeper. His fingers are dangerously close to my other entries, making my nerves light up.

I feel him everywhere, including his warm breath on my neck. The closeness of our bodies only takes me closer as we all but meld together. He braces himself with his arm against the hood of the car, and I fall back onto the hood. We are moving fast now, and every-thing is building. It feels as if the ground is rumbling beneath us, but I know that must be because I am about to lose control.

My vision blurs as I am welcomed with a surge of release. I

scream out his name. A loud boom echoes across the property just as Ry pulls out, exploding himself onto my stomach, my breasts, my neck, making a mess of me.

If there were a noise, it's lost to me. I can't be sure I hear anything as my ears are only buzzing with the sounds of my ecstasy, and the leaves of the hickory smugly swaying in the distance.

15

REFRESHMENTS

RACINE 1978

For a long while, we just stare at each other, out of breath and in awe with what has just transpired, and outside nonetheless. He hovers above me with one hand on each side of my head. Eyes locked, he pushes the hair sticking to my forehead away and slowly lays a kiss there. The moment of softness in complete contradiction to what we were just doing. I want him to do it again.

Ry pulls me up into him and drops me down off the truck and onto the grass beneath. My legs feel like a Jello mold I once saw my mother attempt to make when I was young. Ry holds one of my arms slightly to steady me. I smile up at him, still coming down from the high, and he returns it with a smirk.

"I'll go get us some refreshments," I say as I adjust my shirt back over myself, finding the neckline completely stretched and misshapen. This one will probably find its way to the dump. Ry nods with a smug look on his face, and I grab my sweats that seem to have found themselves under his red truck.

Walking back to the house, I glance back in his direction as he stands buckling up his belt, all while his eyes bore holes into me.

How completely turned around my life has become. An estate and now this. Whatever *this* may be.

Maybe it's not a bad thing. I have a hard time comprehending it being anything but bad. I've grown to be a true pessimist through and through. That view needs to be changed, because after what just occurred, I feel anything but.

I notice two things when I get in the house. One is the heavy feeling of doom that hangs in the air, making it feel even harder to breathe inside these walls. The mirror off to the side wall, enchanting me with its looming darkness, seems to have tripled in scale.

And second, the basement door is open. Again. The door that just may be the death of me. This time I don't close it, but run past quickly to get to the kitchen. Maybe ignoring it will magically make it close on its own, since it has done such a great job of doing the opposite.

The steel refrigerator commands the kitchen, and I head its way. The water from the tap is not the best, so I've been living off the homemade iced tea that I keep in the fridge. I'm thankful the cupboards were stocked with this Southern staple.

I'm about to head back out when I turn and see Ry standing behind me in the kitchen. Staring at me as if he can't believe I'm real. I know that look because it's the same way I find myself feeling about him. But while my eyes hold all excitement and curiosity, his hold a quiet uneasiness, and a dark knowing that I can't seem to look away from.

I should take that as a warning, especially as I notice how his tattoos have deepened against his already deep skin and those two indents on his forehead have become more pronounced. Unsettling, but his beauty seems even more magnified by it all.

"I put some of the wood by your fireplace." He interrupts my thoughts. "The part of the oak that fell was dead. It should be dry enough to burn tonight," his words coming out silky and warm. "Do you know how to start a fire?"

"No, actually. Perhaps you can show me?" I try to say smoothly, but it comes out rushed and jagged. The implications are very clear, and he quirks a smile at that. Reading the tone behind our words tells me our business with each other is far from finished.

"You won't want one until late tonight, and I can help you with that. That is, if you are OK with my coming over later?" Realizing that maybe we aren't talking about an actual fire after all, I blush and nod. Gently taking my face with his fingertips, he tips my head back by the chin.

"Good," he says, hovering his lips over mine. He then softly runs his tongue over my bottom lip. My heartbeat picks up as he presses his full lips into mine, stealing my breath. Ry pulls back to find my eyes. It's an unnerving way I feel when we are like this. So at ease, and yet so wildly not.

"I need to head home," he breaks the silence. "I'll be over later after I clean up." Automatically my mind goes to him showering. He smirks and heads to the front door, knowing my thoughts all too well. It is then that I remember the door to the basement was open.

"Hey, did you by chance come in and open the basement door for any reason?" I ask. His eyes dilate with a visible rage that he reigns back in quickly.

"No, I didn't," he says in a clipped tone. "And I'd advise you to stay away from it. Your uncle mentioned health hazards down there when he got his estate looked at years ago."

"Oh, OK." I look at him quizzically, wondering why that sounded almost like a lie, and what would cause so much strained emotion if the basement is just a health hazard as he says. He says no more of the subject, taking my submission for just that.

———

I'm drawn back outside to look at the work done on the old oak tree,

Ry leaving with the promise to return later tonight. The sad tree looks rather defeated with a large limb missing.

I put my hand on its bark, feeling a need to feel its roughness under my fingers. I don't get the same feelings from this oak as I do from the hickory. A growing smell evokes something in me I know I can place; soft night blooms muddled with a sense of loneliness that I can't equate to being mine.

I sit with the sadness until it becomes me. Full of sorrow, and grief, and longing. I drop my hand from its surface. I too feel like this old oak. There is something missing that I can't put my finger on. A truth that needs to be known. I shake it off, putting distance between me and the tree, thinking maybe my uncle was actually mad after all. I know I'm starting to feel that way.

I stroll past the cherry tree, countless cypress trees and the beautiful magnolia that stands guard of the house. Looking at the tree conjures up my friend, and I realize I should call Lollie to tell her about recent events. Mostly, I tell Lollie everything about my sexual endeavors. However, there is something so all-encompassing about this past one that makes me think I need to keep it to myself.

Regardless if I tell Lollie or not, I long to hear her cheerful voice. My steps echo against the floor on my way to reach for the receiver. I am stopped by a slight breeze. The basement door still stands open as I remember I didn't have the nerve to close it earlier. It seems open wider than before, challenging me.

I hesitantly walk toward it and look down the steps. It doesn't look like anything remarkable, but every hair on my body stands on end, and nervous goosebumps litter my arms. This feeling is starting to be a common occurrence, and at this spot in particular.

Could there be something for me to discover in the darkness of the stairwell? And do I want to find out? My gut says no, so I listen. But still I stare. And when I look down upon the third step, there it is. A purple thistle flower placed perfectly in its center as if it were just for me.

Chills crawl through me as I slam the door and place a large chair in front of it. My heart, pumping blood furiously through me. I am so irked that I forget about calling Lollie and all but run upstairs, praying that a bath will calm my nerves.

I pace back and forth as the water fills the tub. How could a flower have ended up there? Could Carya have brought it in? But she hasn't been outside.

When the steaming water reaches over half, I eventually slide in, letting the warmth of the bubbly liquid ease my worries. I submerge myself in the water, going under into its tranquil depths. I'm greeted by stillness surrounding me completely, doing its job of muting any intrusive thoughts. Relaxation washes over me, and with that mellow, I think of the events that occurred this morning.

My face warms when the thought of Ry pops into my mind. His body and aura, a clear attraction I cannot comprehend. Not only that, but I am no stranger to free love in this day and age. And even if Ry is not feeling the same things that I am, I will live and hope my heart can retain some sort of neutrality.

But could I ever feel this way about someone else? Is this just infatuation being felt by a naïve young woman only just now opening herself to these types of notions? I'm certain it's more.

I step out of the tub and reach for a towel. Prickles of cold shivers fall over my whole body, causing me to snatch the towel of the old brass hook. I wrap it to cover my front, looking around in alarm. I cannot shake the sense of unsteadiness that still floods me. A nagging sensation of being watched sits at my back. I know I am alone, but I am wrong.

At the window, a lone crow sits perched on the branch closest to the bathroom. That sensation gets stronger as I look the bird in the eye. An eye that sparkles with a moonlit glow. Could this be the same bird that interrupted us under the hickory?

It flies off, and I can't help but laugh to myself in the nervous silence. *Real nice Jade...afraid of a bird.* And it is then—I feel utterly pathetic after that.

16

THE FIRE

RACINE 1978

Ry comes over at seven pm sharp, and he is dressed just as sharp. His rich chestnut hair is slicked back, wearing dark slim slacks and a buttoned-down dress shirt. The first three buttons are undone, showing off even more skin art beneath.

He doesn't care about trends. His style is timeless, like a mix of all the best looks over the centuries. He peers at me with a quirked mouth, and if looks could kill, I'd be dead and buried. Or maybe dragged straight to hell, judging by the scars on his forehead. And if I were religious, I'd be reciting the Lord's Prayer right about now.

I'm wearing a mini herringbone shift dress that is the most comfortable one I own. Picking it partly for that reason, but also because of how flattering it is on me. I painted my lips a dusty salmon pink, and Ry's eyes go to them first, then to my legs. There it is. That intensity. That want. That spark that could put the whole fucking room up in flames.

Ry walks straight toward me; he takes one strand of my hair and loops it around his finger.

"How have I gone so long without this feeling of you? Whatever you are putting out...it's suffocating. But in a good way. Try to tell me you don't feel that, too?" He murmurs in my ear, and the air between us shifts. Speaking the answers to my own questions with the urgency of his.

Not finding the words, I nod at his vulnerability. I think how morbid his description of us is, but also how it is exactly right. He cocks his head to the side at my lack of response.

"Let's get you a fire going. I need you verbal." He says with a wink, and my thighs clench close as my thoughts drift to the reason.

I watch him silently build a fire, and as it roars to life, so does something inside me. Something known, but hidden. Something primal, but calm—for now, at least. I have never felt this stirring from within before, but it pulls me closer to Ry. A warning? I ignore it.

I kneel and place my hand on Ry's shoulder as he crouches down by the fire. His head turns, and he places his hand on top of mine. His eyes are questions burning into me. Asking if I know? If I can feel it, too?

He takes my cheek in his hands, and gone is the rough man from earlier. He moves closer so our lips graze each other's. Although barely there physically, the electricity jumps between us like sparks dancing between flames in a fire, a heady sense of what comes next. We may not have the answers, but I think he will do his best to make sure I feel them.

He runs his tongue along my top lip and then his mouth is on mine, grasping a handful of my hair. He wraps his hand around my lower waist and eases me down onto the hardwood floor, just warming up from the fireplace blazing beside us.

This feels concrete. Something about these moments solidifying a bond that is inevitable. He surrounds me as he places his elbows on each side of my body and sinks closer into me, breathing me in.

This rush of him on top of me is one I want to savor, and his hands—his hands everywhere. I want them everywhere, and I feel myself arching up into the hardness of him, causing him to release a low groan. The sound is something much like a melody of all my favorite songs combined, which I now know happen to be his favorite, too.

"Open your legs for me, Jade," he demands. At that moment, my shift dress has moved its way up to my waist, leaving my lower half completely exposed, including my panty-less bottom. An invitation. I know exactly when Ry notices, because his eyes darken.

"Did you do this just for me?" He asks, but he knows. "How absolutely succulent you are." He hums the words in my ear.

I giggle in response, and his hand goes in between us to the spot that has been aching for him since this morning. He glides two fingers inside, and I gasp, needing more. Wanting him. All of him. He takes his fingers out of me and brings them to his mouth, sucking them clean. I watch with fascination. Did he really just taste me?

Anticipation being my favorite part of this journey, we've only just now started exploring. He undoes his pants and pulls himself out. Rubbing himself against me. My body answers him before I can. Ry takes himself to my center and pushes just his tip into me, stretching me out, but I want more. I need more.

I wrap my legs around his torso and flip him over. It's not graceful, but desire never is. The mess is half the fun. I slide down onto his full length, and he stretches me out as I ride up and down. He squeezes my thighs so hard I know there will be bruises in the morning. I can feel them forming now, but I want to wear all the marks of him, on my skin and on my heart.

As I move up and down, my mind flashes to a young woman putting on the ring from the jade willow. Is that me? Her world spins, and then she jumps off the banister. I gasp, my body falling back into the waves of ecstasy.

I forget the brief glimpse into the past as I focus on the sensations building within my core. Then, Ry is sitting up while I continue to straddle him. My nipple meets his hot, wet mouth. I arch and I moan. No, this is my favorite part.

"Fuck," I rasp out.

"There are those words I was looking for. Say more, sweetheart. I want to hear you swear to me as you come around my cock," he says as he peers up at me.

I look at him. His pupils blown wide, his gaze wild and hungry. I see him then, in a different time, wearing a soldier's uniform, handing a girl a ring in the alley. That must be me again. Her face so similar but different. Younger.

His lips come for mine. Something about our mouths and tongues moving together, mimicking what is happening lower between us as he pushes into me, has me coming undone.

"Oh, God!" The scream releases from my lips as my sensitive insides spasm around him.

"I can be that for you. It's not too far off." Ry whispers in my ear as I shudder into him.

He spins me around and lifts my hips up, so my hands fall and meet the ground. My knees find it shortly after, and that's when he pushes into me from behind. I am soaked with want, with all my most sensitive nerves screaming for him to move his dick in and out, faster and harder.

Now, I see Ry in my mind's eye. Standing before me, but morphing into a tree as a hawk circles above him. Back and forth he goes. Man to tree. Tree to man.

He pounds me from behind. I am still sensitive from my orgasm, so it feels like everything I would want it to. Ry continues pumping, while grasping my behind in his large palm. He smacks it, which makes me scream, and I feel myself close to the edge again.

He moves faster and faster, and the Ry of my vision comes back. Man to tree. Tree to man. Man to hickory. *Hickory.*

At that realization, I am lost to the feelings of my needy body again. Ry grunts, and I know he is coming apart as much as I am. He falls forward above me and wraps his arm around, so his hand palms my breast and the other one lays flat on the ground holding him up.

"Oh, my love, how I've missed you," he says in heavy breaths.

"From just this morning?" I question, but now unwrapping a truth that was hidden from me before. Seeing Ry as someone completely different. *Something*. Hickory, I think, trying to piece the last puzzle part together.

"Since before either of us knew." His sure remark places a permanent stitch in my heart. And any silly disillusionment of what my visions played out dissipates.

We fall in an exhausted heap of limbs onto the floor. And that's when I know his touch has woven into the very fiber of me, like trees growing too close—entwined, tangled, beautiful. Dangerous, even as one could so easily choke out the other. But that won't happen to us.

FLASHBACK
SCOTLAND 1416

It started with a rip in my apron. A rip that led me to make an unexpected trip into town to spend my wages on an unnecessary expense: thread, a needle, and extra fabric in case it tore again. Getting into town is mostly done on foot if you are of lower status, such as myself, which proves to be a two-day journey. So, you have to hope the weather is in your favor.

I work for the lord of a castle that sits just behind the English border in Scotland. Although poor, I have more than many. So, I find myself in no position to complain.

The first day of travel is near perfect weather, but that doesn't last. As my luck has it, the next day changes into a torrential downpour. Rain comes out of nowhere, so I take cover under a large hickory tree to wait it out. While I sit there, I collect some of its nuts that have fallen to the ground, knowing I will need more nourishment on the rest of my journey that may turn longer due to the given circumstances.

A lone thistle plant sits in the nook of a protruding root of this old hickory, and I can't help but examine its purple flower. The petals themselves are a drastic contrast to the rest. Thistle is bountiful here, and mostly used by the locals to ward off evil around one's home.

My mother thought otherwise. She warned me of the so-called devil's plant that lured one in with its bright purple bud, only to pierce your skin if you got too close. She said that if it did happen to make you bleed, the devil would have ownership over your soul.

My mother was full of these tales, handed down through centuries of tradition and religion. I didn't believe in such things, but I didn't let her know. To appease her, I told her I would never touch one.

My mother wasn't here now though, and curiosity does always have a way of getting the best of me, especially within the boredom of the monsoon coming down everywhere except my protected canopy. I carefully go to stroke one of the thorny leaves and am poked almost instantly. Sharp little buggers.

A drop of blood falls down my finger, and I wipe it away on the grass at the base of the tree. It barely hurts, and the clouds didn't darken over me, which I'll take as a good sign. Just as I suspected, my mother's tales were a bunch of rubbish.

I wait under the tree for what seems like half the day when finally, a carriage comes by. It stops before me, a hand reaching out its window to wave me over. With my bonnet tight around my face, I make my way over to the carriage and the mysterious hand that beckoned me.

The door opens as an invitation. I step inside, thankful to get out of the rain. You can never not heed someone of higher ranking, so it wasn't much of a question of what my next steps would be when invited into such a blessed opportunity like this.

Once I wipe the rain from my lashes, I glance up to show my good graces to the person extending their kindness to me, but I am left without words. Before me is the most bonnie lad with dark brown hair. Two faint scars mark his forehead, but they don't distract from his beauty in the least. He doesn't look much older than me, so I can not believe my luck.

I finally get my words about me, and thank the man who reaches his hand out to me. This is an unexpected action, because a man of his status would never acknowledge a lowly servant girl like me. But I oblige, and the moment I do, I never look back as he places a soft kiss against my knuckles.

"What is your name, sir?" I fumble out. It is the only thing I can think to ask.

"Carya, although some call me Hickory. You, my little succulent, can call me Ry." You would think his nickname referring to my name would make me uneasy, but it does the opposite. It feels undeniably natural. The only unnerving part about it is how he knows my name to make a nickname of it? Maybe it is merely a coincidence.

"My name is Jade." I announce, even though he shows no signs of asking.

"I know," is all he says after. I should be unsettled, but that reaction doesn't reach me. Instead, I stare unapologetically the entire way to town. Quiet and unassuming in our study of each other. A reciprocation I feel in every part of my being.

I do not know many in town apart from the shop owners I visit when I come here every other month for supplies. However, it seems as if all eyes are on me today. Or maybe not me, but focusing on the man who takes my hand, directing me through town as if he were my own personal escort.

I stop into the seamstress shop and grab what I need, while the gentleman waits outside for me. Why he waits for me I cannot fathom, but I am not about to object to his forward attention. That is until I hear the whispers of the women in the shop. Something about the Englishman.

English. His accent. I should've known. I didn't even think to ask what he is doing here, but I see now the crest he wears. The crest that shows his loyalty to King Henry.

My lord would fire me immediately if he found out I was conversing with an Englishman. I decide to let him know we will have to part ways when I leave the shop. I look at him directly as people passing by still look at us in disgust, so I bring him into an alley.

"I greatly appreciate your gesture towards me, but I must be on my own now." I say in the most respectable manner I can muster up.

"Is that so?" he smirks. Oh, those lips. I blush at my meddlesome thought. My gaze trails to his neck, mostly hidden beneath his coat. Strange markings just barely showing under his buttoned collar.

"It wouldn't be because of the crest I bear on my jacket, would it? Oh, Jade, I thought you would be a little more rebellious this time around, not care about what a few townspeople thought." He looks disappointed and seems to mock me. And this time around? What could he mean by that?

"Well, I'm afraid my job is at stake here, and the good name of my family, so I must bid you farewell." I say and go to leave. Having already gotten what I need in town, I am about to find a place to stay for the night before my journey back to the castle. But before I can leave, I am pulled back into the alley.

Eyes matching the color of the loch waters bore into my soul. They almost seem full of panic and pleading. Asking me a question. They invoke a sense of instinct. An instinct to give everything to the man in front of me.

He places a small object into my palm at that moment. A ring.

"Please remember, Jade. Here. I made this for you. I need you to remember us." He pleads and then adds, "I didn't go all this way across the realms to get here, just for you to walk through this world blindly. Please put this on." His sadness confuses me, and it confuses me even more when I look up to ask him what this is, but he is gone.

I feel floaty after that interaction and promptly go find a room, needing to avoid the onlookers from earlier today and to be alone with my thoughts. How dare I be so dense not to notice the crest he wore?

Was I really so enamored with the way he looked that I would overlook such an important detail? Of course, I was. I am only twenty, and I despise saying it, but the thought of such a beautiful man showing me any ounce of attention should not be my fault. Although there are names for women who disgrace their purity in such a way.

The sun fades in the room I bought with the only coin left to my name. My mind won't rest as the man from today consumes my every thought. I pretend we didn't have to say farewell that night, and give in to desires that would make most girls blush.

I am no longer in control. Only the man with the angst in his eyes has control over me now. His invisible claim on my body, quietly guiding my thistle-pricked fingers, bringing myself to bliss. The devil's plant she warned. I'm glad I didn't listen.

I imagine it now. His lips on my neck, soft but urgent. I dip my hand lower, grazing my belly, and follow the path to my most delicate parts. He is there now, licking and sucking until I'm sure he is in this very room with me. I open my eyes for just a moment. Shadows twirl about me. Surely stars brought on for what comes next.

Two fingers find their way inside me. They are mine, but they don't feel that way. Who truly guides me to this point? The smell of woody earth and burning hickory envelops me. I did not make a fire, but there is one starting within.

I choke on the dense earthy smell as I hit the spot that ached so deeply for the English soldier. My insides pulse, and I ride the soft waves surrounding my fingers as I make a wet mess of them. A proper woman would be ashamed, but it is not my fault—for the devil took over tonight.

When I am done, I think about the devil's plant beneath that old hickory. I wonder if perhaps there was something to my mother's warnings after all. The tiny prick throbs more intensely as I think of it now.

I am rather not myself since meeting the man in the carriage. The one who showed up just moments after a pinpoint of blood appeared on my finger. But a mere coincidence is no reason to believe in superstitions now. I believe only in what I experienced today, which was cut short by the sad reality of political disputes.

———

The ring stays snugly in my pocket until I finally make my way back to the castle. There isn't much time to think about it once I get back. I work all day, and only rest when the sun goes down. The downside of being of inferior status. My tired feet hold a constant ache that shouldn't belong at my young age.

I have a small and dark dirt room in the castle. A basic servant's quarters, and that is where I go to mend the hole in my apron. I pull out the needle and thread, and with it comes the ring. It is quite a lovely ring, one made of metal and stone I have never seen before. One that speaks of wealth and power, and I know nothing of that.

Against my better judgement, I place the ring upon my finger. A perfect fit. The walls close in around me as I am pulled into memories. But my heart can't take what I see.

I see a young Romanian woman being swallowed by the earth as a dark male figure greets her. It is me. Branches grow out of his head. His lips taste of victory and remorse as he lays a kiss against me. And then, his hand is against my throat as roots impale my skin and my blood drains beneath the base of an old hickory.

My soul cannot do this again. I cry through the night, and by dawn, I find release the only way I can—looping the leftover fabric into a noose, and I let myself fall off the banister of the castle's main entry. Whoever finds me, the Gods bless them.

17

RECORD SHOP

RACINE 1978

We wake in each other's arms, somehow having made it from the fire to the stairway to my bed. The sheets are wrapped around us in a way that is telling of what took place last night. Ry's fingers find my face, trailing lightly along the profile of my nose, ending his journey on my bottom lip. He pushes down and rubs it like he can't believe it is there. As quickly as his thumb is there, he then replaces it with his lips, and I welcome it wholeheartedly.

"Let me take you to breakfast," he says, almost more of a demand than an inquiry.

"You must read minds," I murmur. Slightly smiling as I stretch my arms above my head.

We dress quickly. He is in the clothes from the night before, looking more than disheveled, while I jump into a pair of bell bottom jeans and a light grey button-down collared shirt. Before we head out the door, he looks at me in a way that says too much without uttering a single word. Maybe I look that way too, because we both stare at each other like there is only us in this world. For all I care, we are.

But soon, his eyes lose their sparkle as his gaze turns hopeless. I can't figure out his emotions and what they mean, but I do feel them.

And they feel much like a story I've been told before. Much like everything in this house. Much like everything about Ry. And I really want to know why.

———

It takes twenty-five minutes to get into town. We go back to *The Spanish Moss*, which is quickly becoming my favorite place to dine out. Their breakfast outdoes anything we have in Detroit. I make sure Walt and Cattie know. Detroit has its own charm, but a bayou breakfast hits different.

"I need to run some quick errands," Ry says to me as we are standing by the little table set near the window. "There are some shops you may want to browse in the meantime."

"Oh, OK. I guess I did see a couple on the way in." I say, not wanting to separate our time together just yet, but also intrigued to see some more of what this town has to offer in terms of shops.

"I'll meet you on this block in forty-five minutes. Do you have a watch?" Ry asks, pointing to his wrist.

"I do." I answer, pursing my lips and instinctively touching the wrist that holds my mother's watch, which has remained a staple item in my daily wardrobe ever since she passed.

Ry grabs my attention then. He softly grasps my upper arm and stares into my eyes like he wants to kiss me, but decides against it. That one hesitation tells me everything and makes me question what I really am to him.

But his choice won't defeat me. For a minute I let myself dream we could be more than just a casual convenience, but that was my own wishful thinking. Just a delusional girl making things more than they are.

I become angry with myself for not having more experience in these types of situations. The idea that maybe he doesn't want his friends seeing us kiss crosses my mind now that I notice them peering from behind the kitchen door.

Gone are their kind faces. Their eyes come off a bit prying, to be honest. Perhaps this town is all too eager to know and spread the business of the young lawyer and a newly inherited estate owner after all. And maybe he has been through this before with someone else, and he had to learn the lesson the hard way?

"What a crappy hand we've been dealt." Ry says under his breath, looking at the owners. This moment of vulnerability—rare and confusing. I don't know for whom it is intended, and I don't want to.

I give Ry a weak smile, and wave to the owners. Suddenly not wanting to be here, I make my way out the door. I turn around thinking Ry will be right behind, but when I glance back, he is gone.

An uncomfortable wrenching feeling graces my chest. I shrug it off, knowing his issues are not mine, and wander the streets of the little bayou town. Heartache of the young and fickle can wait—this town is calling.

I lose track of time on these sunny streets, too busy weaving in and out of darling shops. After going into an antique store and a tiny used bookstore, I finally find myself rooted in a record shop. I am downright giddy to have found it, and I can't resist browsing through their vast selection of records without a care in the world. Everything from Billie Holiday to Fleetwood Mac to Neil Young lives here amongst these shelves.

I feel right at home, and so immersed that I don't register the person beside me. I feel his presence before I even look up, and when I do, I am greeted by acorn-brown eyes with a moonlit ring around them. And to my surprise, he is staring straight at me.

I jump and step back, startled because I recognize these eyes and this face. The same man from outside that bar in Detroit—the one who vanished like a dream.

"Why, aren't *you* a gem to behold..." Breaking out of his spell, I scoff up at him.

"Excuse me," I say, and I drift to the other side of the record aisle.

His stare remains intense and unfaltering. I keep my head down, but I feel his eyes roaming over me. He doesn't acknowledge me as if we've met before, so perhaps this isn't the same man. And why would he be in this town anyway? I was fairly intoxicated that night, so I cannot be entirely sure.

He continues watching me, and just when I think I can't escape his unearthly gaze any longer, a cheery girl pops to my side and speaks.

"Can I help you with something? Or at least get this annoying pest of a man out of your space?" She exclaims, flashing her white teeth at me. Joking, I think.

I look between her and the man. She looks unfazed and a bit mischievous. And him...well, I would think her comment bore him, if it weren't for the flash of flustered annoyance that crosses his face.

"Oh boy," the girl looks from me to the man and back to me again. "I hope Que isn't bothering you. He's harmless really. I'm Cher. I work here. And Que is..."

"Leaving." He says as if he couldn't be bothered. And he walks past me, brushing shoulders. I turn to look back just as he does, and we lock eyes. It's only for a second, unnatural white blonde hair contrasting against his dark eyebrows, and then he turns his head back to the front door before he leaves the store entirely.

"Oh, don't mind him. He is always like that," says Cher, but I can't put my finger on what *that* is.

"So, are you from out of town? I can't say I've seen you around here before. Most people who come into the shop are locals, *always* nice to see a new face." Her question getting lost in her ramblings.

"Um, actually, I recently inherited a house about twenty-five minutes from here. It was my uncle's..." Her eyes open wide, intrigued to know more, glossing them over.

"Don't tell me you are talking about The Rooted Realm Estate?" She says with equal shock and curiosity.

"Yeah, that's the one," I respond, trying to wrap my head around why everyone knows about my apparently infamous estate.

"Oh, my goodness! My mother used to tell me about that place. Apparently, your uncle put together some pretty magnificent balls. People from all over Louisiana would come to them. You *must* have me over. Oh, I would just love to see that place!" She rattles on about the extravagant old parties before catching herself.

"Oh no, I am *so* sorry. I didn't even realize. I am being way too forward, and you lost your uncle just recently. I am so sorry." I try to speak, but it's no use as she continues on, "Sometimes, I can be a bit dense. I didn't mean to carry on so. This damn overactive brain of mine." She takes a deep breath then, and I wonder if I'll ever get a word in. "I am so sorry for your loss, and for overstepping my boundaries."

"It's OK, really," I say at last. And I mean it. There is something about Cher I find reassuring. She's a little like Lollie, but with a hint of something wilder.

"Actually, I didn't know him at all. And to be honest, it would be nice to have someone to visit me. If you are indeed interested, that is..." I ask. She all but jumps with excitement and tells me she can't wait.

We schedule a time for later tonight before I realize what a crazy idea this is to invite someone over whom I've only met mere seconds ago. I add it to my list of risks, and leave the record shop with a new friend, a dinner to plan, and even a couple new records.

Ry pulls up to the corner, and I climb in.

"There you are," he says. "How was roaming around?"

"Great, actually." I say with a big smile brimming on my face, "I may need to stop at the grocery store as well, if that's alright?" I ask, thinking about what to make tonight, knowing my kitchen skills are less than par.

"I can do that. Big plans then? I should tell you I have a couple meetings later, so I won't make it over your way." He says, as if expecting he would be the only reason for my plans.

"That's alright. I have a friend coming over. Just met her. Cher." At the sound of her name, Ry's shoulders straighten, and the relaxed expression he was wearing morphs into something serious and grave.

"Oh, OK, I wasn't aware Cher was back in town." He is tight-lipped suddenly, but then continues, "Some people in this town are not always how they come across at first. Be careful Jade. I wouldn't want you to be fooled, especially by her." He says darkly.

I'm suddenly feeling oddly defensive of Cher, and annoyed that this man thinks he has any say in whom I converse with, especially if he can't even acknowledge us in front of his friends.

"Well, let's leave that up to me to decide, thank you. Do you two have a history or something?" I ask, genuinely curious.

"Only the kind that I'd rather not have anymore." He says cryptically. What is he hiding? My walls go up. Warning bells I should have heard weeks ago are ringing clear.

"That's a pretty immature response. Do you care to expand on that?" I ask now very irked by his lack of clarity. His shoulders relax as if giving in to whatever internal battle is raging within him.

"I know this sounds irrational, but she has too many opinions about...things in my life. People who are meant to be *mine*—I mean in my life." He snarls in disgust, then adds, "Plus, she keeps the worst company. That's really all I want to say on the matter." He closes off then, red flags swirling all around me. Could he be referring to Que?

"Well, thank you for opening up," I respond, realizing he really gave me nothing to go on. But I don't push after that, because I really don't care to hear him talk. Men and their egos. I look out the window for the rest of the trip. We drive to the grocery store and then home. Not one word is spoken until we pull up to my house.

"I'll call you," I say, and leave him lacking. If we're playing games, I'll hold my pride too.

18

DINNER PARTY

RACINE 1978

My mother was never one for hosting. She was a self-proclaimed hermit, and that trait seemed to pass along to me with ease. However, I find my excitement about having a friend come over is palpable. In preparation, I made all the things I hoped would make for an enjoyable meal. A cheese plate with olives. Spaghetti with meatballs and dark chocolate brownies for dessert, because if I know how to do one thing, it's bake.

The oven goes off right as the doorbell rings and sounds through the thick walls of the relic estate that I now call a home. It must be an old Southern house quirk. The way sound reverberates through everything, but it still spooks me every time.

I hurry to the door after pulling the warm treats out of the oven so they have time to cool. The moment I open it, I am greeted by an overly bright smile from Cher. Her smile holds an ounce of apology, because behind her stands a very tall and very amused man. Que. And the smirk on his face tells me he is very pleased to have found his way in on our dinner date.

"We're here!" Cher sings brightly.

"Ah, yes, we're..." I say as I dart my eyes to Que, but look away instantly because his eyes were already on me.

"I found Que wandering the streets on my way here, and he just looked so pitiful. I hope you don't mind my dragging him along. He could really use a dinner among friends instead of one of his late-night ladies for a change." Que clears his throat at her bluntness, and I nearly trip over my next words.

"Oh," I blush and speak again, "Uh, yes, that's no problem. We should have plenty of food."

Earning a sideways glance from Cher's uninvited friend, I walk them to the library and hand them each a glass of red wine. Apart from the liquor, the wine was a little harder to come across at the estate. A couple of bottles sat undisturbed in the bottom cupboard of the pantry with a note most likely written by my uncle. The writing is neat and clear—unexpected from someone said to suffer from mental ailments.

It read, 'must retrieve more,' but retrieve from where is the question. My first guess would be the basement, but a resounding no is all I hear when I think of traveling down those cold, damp steps. I made a unanimous decision that the bottles up here would have to do for the night.

"The wine is quite good," a nonchalant male voice breaks the silence. "I'm detecting notes of oak," Que grins. Any other man saying that statement would make me cringe, but he says it rather mockingly, like a one-sided joke only he gets.

"Que knows his way around a wine cellar," chimes Cher. "He actually traveled the world and brought back a bottle from each place he has visited. He let me tag along for a couple. Quite an adventure. We traveled all along the Balkan Mountains, France...oh, and Scotland."

"Wow, that sounds like quite an adventure indeed. So, you two are a couple then?" I ask, hoping not to come off too nosy. Cher's eyes widen in horror, and then her boisterous laughter rings through the room. Making my question sound like one of the funniest things she has heard in her life.

"Oh *God,* no!!" Cher voices through tears of laughter. Que is looking at Cher with a smirk of adoration and then to me, but I turn my eyes quickly toward Cher as she continues, "Que is just my oldest, dearest friend. We grew up together. We've been through a lot of life's big events, so we have a bit of an unwritten pact of sorts. Like —siblings, I guess." She ponders that for a moment before she continues,

"Although I think if we were siblings, we would've killed each other a long time ago." And with that, she bursts out laughing again. Her laugh is infectious, and I find myself pulled into it, smiling along.

"So, what is your favorite part of this house so far, Jade?" Que pulls my attention away as he looks me dead on. "I hear this place makes quite an impression on people. Your uncle being one of them. Mad as a hatter, they would say." Que says it as if it were a fact.

"I'm not sure about my uncle. To be honest, I didn't know him." I look to Que, trying to get a read on him. I would expect to take offense at his comment about the uncle I never knew, but he says it as if it were just a natural occurrence.

"I suppose the property is my favorite part. There is an old willow by the water I'm quite fond of. But mostly, I like the stillness of it all here. The house. The property. It just...is." I admit, realizing my tongue led me to be more sincere that I would like.

I look around, bashful at my openness. But I am not met with judgement. As I look at these two dinner guests, who are strangers really, only empathy sits at this dinner table. Especially Que, who eyes me with intention. The spell is broken quickly.

"Let's hear more of your thoughts about the other trees. I bet there is quite a variety here, including a famed oak. Rumor has it, it's well over five hundred years old. Right, Cher?" And they look at each other in an oddly deceiving way. I find it hard to believe that a tree on the estate would be on anyone's radar for town gossip. But, this is a strange place.

"There *is* a big, old oak. Massive really. A large limb broke the other day. It took out one of the other trees near it during the storm last week." With my declaration of that fact, or maybe it was when the word 'oak' came out of my mouth, Que's moon-colored ring around his iris flashed an iridescent twinkle impossible to miss.

"Imagine that." Que says, looking at me intensely. Cher breaks the silence by smacking her red lips together. A sure hint to keep the mood light.

We change the topic to Cher's work at the record shop. It's a lighter conversation, and I find out she has just moved back to town from an extended vacation. Her record shop being on a bit of a sabbatical until now.

Hungry and sightly tipsy, we make our way to the dinner table, piling food high on our plates. Charm oozes from both of them as if they've practiced wooing newcomers their whole lives. And every once in a while, I find Que's eyes locked on mine, which makes my skin tingle.

I could go without that added reaction, having enough on my plate with Ry's confusing advances. I don't want to like it, but he is exceptionally handsome. It would be odd if I didn't find it at least a little pleasing.

By the time we finish eating, we are feeling quite good from the two bottles of wine that now sit empty, littered across the dining table.

"Oh, shoot. Looks like we are out of wine," Cher pouts, her mouth making somewhat of a dramatic statement with full lips stained a wine-colored cherry hue.

"I could only find the two bottles upstairs. I'm sure there are more somewhere around here, but I haven't had the nerve to venture around to look very hard for them." I say, and I realize the wine is making my lips looser than I would like.

I am loving this company, but something sets me on edge about the way Cher and Que seem to know things about the property and even about my uncle, for that matter. All dinner they've been spilling little facts and secrets like they know more than the average towny.

And then, Que stands with mischief in his eyes.

"Well, shall we?" He holds his hand out to me.

"Shall we what?" I ask a bit confused and off balance by the sudden change of sitting down version of Que, to him towering over me in his full height. He isn't the tallest man, maybe six foot at best, but charisma oozes off him and must add at least two feet of allure. An allure that he knows most women respond eagerly to.

"Well, we are out of wine, and I imagine there is a wine cellar is this massive estate. So, shall we have a look around?" He says to me in such a casual way, you would think we've known each other for years.

"Oh, yes, please!" Cher declares, looking to me, her eyes ecstatic. "I am in need of more libations!" She stands up, but wobbles a bit, obviously feeling the effects of the numerous glasses she has drunk already. I find her choice of words humorous, coming from a time that doesn't quite fit this one.

"Well, I guess maybe I should sit this one out. I'll stay here with the brownies while you two look. Please and thank you!" I giggle at how she speaks, or maybe it is from the fact that I too have had more than a few glasses.

Because of this giggle, I almost miss the look Cher directs toward the charming man beside me. It's an omniscient look that passes between the two of them. And before I can make much of it, I am whisked out of my chair by my arm and dragged toward the base-ment—feeling pleased that I slipped off my heels under the table before I was stolen out of my seat to look for the lost wine. Otherwise, I would be tripping all over myself even more so than I already am.

Que keeps dragging me forward hand in hand and looks back every once in a while to shoot a mischievous look. I'm feeling overly bubbly and welcoming of his overwhelming presence. His manner having a way of slowly growing on me.

That is until we come to the basement door.

"Oh no, I don't think they would be down there." I exclaim, knowing my words taste untruthful and are based more in fear than anything else.

"You *do* know that most wine cellars are in basements. I truly doubt you are that dense," Que says and crooks his eyebrow at me like he can see through my facade.

"True, but not in Louisiana...In fact, I'm very curious how there is even one here at all. It can't be safe. Probably flooded..." I say, trying to sound like I know what I'm talking about.

"Ah, yes. But this is a very curious house. Things that shouldn't be—are. Or so I've heard..." After his unsettling remark, Que opens the door.

A stale and musty air blows my hair back, tickles my shoulders, and makes my stomach drop. I tense at the feeling of the old, cool breeze against my skin, but it seems as if Que is feeding off of its energy. He looks taller, bolder, and even more enchanting, if that can even be possible.

Que eyes me then, and oh, that look. Nobody should be the owner of such a look. My stomach falls further, but this time into a scattering of butterflies. And even more so when Que remarks with a lick of his lips and a wink of his eye.

"Don't worry, I'll hold your hand," he says, and with that comment, I would follow him to the edge of the world.

I guess it's decided then, because my legs involuntarily follow his as I'm whisked away by his offer. Weaving my fingers through his in a vice grip, we cautiously move down the steps into what I can only imagine is a very unstable foundation. There are small scones that light the way down, and Que turns each one on with a twist as if he has done it a million times before.

The air gets heavier and earthier the farther we move down the steps. The smell of moss clings to my nostrils, making an impenetrable barrier, so I can smell only that. I attribute it to the depth of the basement itself, as if we were walking farther and farther into the earth's core.

Que's Oxford clad feet move casually down with one hand in his pant pocket and one holding tightly to my own. Whereas I can barely see in front of me, Que must have super vision because he hasn't missed a step and seems to know exactly where his foot placement needs to be to carry us all the way down. And down we go. We must have traveled at least thirty steps at this point. *Impossible.*

At the bottom of the steps, I am left out of breath, still clasping tightly to Que. The floor is cement, making it colder down here as if we were in a century-old crypt. The chills move from the back of my neck and into the center of my shoulder blades. Que must realize this and sweeps his arm around me, guarding me from the chill gracefully dancing around us. Not an ounce of water floods these floors, making my head spin.

"Now this is a basement that definitely holds fine wine," and he looks down at me with a smug smile that shows the subtlest dimple in his cheek. His hair seems to shine a beaming metallic white glow as if reflecting a full moon that doesn't exist in these depths.

In fact, the mere lack of light glowing off the scones could not possibly be enough to make him gleam the way he does right now. Even so, I feel a little more comfortable in his presence as he moves us toward a wide and open entry with no door. Beside the entry sits a small table that has a candle sconce having a look that belongs to a few centuries before ours.

"Would you mind lighting this, love?" He asks. It sounds so very enduring and easy coming off his lips, and I can hear a hint of an accent I hadn't noticed before.

"Oh, sure," I say absentmindedly, and I pull out the lighter I keep for my cloves. How he assumes I have a lighter floats through my mind. He doesn't know I smoke, but the memory of a mysterious man outside a bar comes back. That had to be him then, right? And as if he can hear my thoughts, I find him studying my reaction.

"Don't worry, gem. We all partake in a smoke here and there." And that's what he leaves me with as he turns and walks into the doorless room.

The room that I thought would be small and dark is actually massive. Light from the candle bounces off mirrors that are placed in odd places along the walls, giving the entire room an expansive, warm glow.

There are huge shelves stuffed full of bottles around the room and lining the walls. Not one wall is spared. I have never seen so much wine in my life, and from the looks of it, some of these bottles are extremely old and rare.

Que strolls to the back, blows off the bottles sitting there, and grabs two.

"Ah, here we are," Que says as he pulls them from their respective cubbies. He knows just where to go, as if he's strolled through this cellar many times before. Placing one in my hand, I see it is indeed the exact bottle we were drinking before.

"Oh, those are the same type..." I look up at him, my eyebrows burrowing together as I try to figure out how he knew those were there, but he doesn't seem to notice—or just doesn't care.

"I figured we didn't need a hangover from mixing any other varieties tonight," he says. He is standing awfully close, and I can feel his eyes on my neck like he wants to take a bite out of it. I'm not sure I would object if he did.

Speaking of my current reserve. Where I once was standoffish to Que's type, I'm finding his special kind of smugness a bit captivating. I just can't shake off this sense that he may know this house better than I do.

And it is not only the wine. I feel it is this place. Every moment in this wine cellar with him harboring a deep curiosity. The longer he is here, the more I feel like he has been here before.

With his free hand, he sweeps one strand of my misplaced hair off my shoulder. The heat left behind by that small action creeps all over the surface of my skin. I do my best to ignore it and look at him, trying to get a hint of the real him.

I see so much emotion from a time past in his eyes. Pain, sadness, all barely being held together by his careless demeanor. It is love he needs. In this moment, I want to perch up on my tiptoes and kiss him. And that is what I do. I give him a quick peck on the top of his nose.

I can see it takes him off guard, because he steps back startled, unconsciously tugging at the bottom of his shirt. It doesn't take him long to find his casual demeanor again when he swings the wine bottle up to rest on his shoulder.

"Well, if you wanted a kiss, we could have made that a whole of a lot better than just a peck," he grins, taking my hand as we walk out of the wine cellar room.

I am a bit surprised at myself for that action, but something about him looked so vulnerable—so *sad*. I wanted to show him a smidge of kindness as opposed to the passion he must constantly receive from women.

"Take what you can get," I say jokingly. His eyes darken then, and he spins around to face me, pushing me against the cold cellar wall. I gasp at the cold shock of it. The warmth from him softens it a bit.

"What I can take as opposed to what I can get are two entirely different notions. And I enjoy taking a lot more. Be careful with that smart mouth of yours." His lips curve into a devilish grin, and his eyes dilate with moonlight. *Oh.*

Fear slices through my body, but it's fear of myself and what I fear I want him to take. But before I can find out, he pushes off the wall and starts back on his way to the steps. It takes a minute for me to regain my composure, and only then do I head toward him—but not too close.

Even though his words were harsh, his impression wasn't. Still, I keep my distance. I see there are a few more doorless rooms, and toward the back there is a larger entry. I walk that way, curiosity getting the best of me.

The smell of damp earth comes full force, assaulting my senses the closer I get. And it is far. I feel like I am walking across the whole of the estate property in this vast basement. Time doesn't seem to hold value inside these concrete walls. I feel myself lost in it.

Just when I think I'm getting closer to the door, a hand grabs me and pulls me back. It is Que. He looks unhinged and even bigger. *How does he keep growing?*

"No need for exploring tonight, little gem," Que says, and I am unapologetically dragged upstairs, back to the dinner table with no answers to the distant room I was about to discover.

Cher is cleaning up the table and seems a bit more sober, which I'm sure she will be happy about come morning.

"What the hell were you two doing? You were gone forever," she says in a cheerful, singsong voice. "I've cleaned up everything and put the leftovers in the kitchen. Que, we must leave. I am feeling absolutely dreadful after all that wine." If she feels that way, she doesn't sound it.

"Oh, we just grabbed more wine. How about you take one home?" I chime in, suddenly wanting them to be on their way. "There is more wine down there than I will ever need in this lifetime."

"But what about the next?" Cher makes the odd remark. I look at her confused. "Oh, I mean the next time we visit. But if you insist, I will take it. Also, I'm afraid I need Que here to drive me home as soon as possible before I pass out on that wingback over there." With that, Que quickly grabs his coat and hers, helping his friend to the door.

"Thank you so much for coming." I give Cher a quick peck on the cheek, but am not sure how to send off Que with how the basement scenario had just played out minutes before.

"Come back again," I stutter, and in an unsure manner add, "Both of you."

"Oh, I will, Jade," Que says rather matter-of-factly. Cher sends a smile that says more than I can read. And then they are just simply out the door.

The nights are getting stranger and stranger in this small Louisiana town that, in all honesty, I could barely find on the map driving here. This place could be an illusion for all I know. The way it plays tricks on my sanity makes me think I'm not far off.

19

HIDDEN DOORS

RACINE 1978

It feels as if a boulder lay on top of my head the next morning. Drinking always comes with a bit of regret and a long road to recovery. I refuse to get out of bed for most of the day, and can only muster up enough energy to have a glass of water and a small piece of toast. Afterward, I promptly crawl back, disappearing beneath the mass of cloud-like cover.

The next time I wake up, the phone is ringing, and the sun is slowly making its descent on the other side of the sky. Reluctantly, I pull myself out of bed to make my way downstairs. My legs like lead posts behind me, not quite able to catch up to the rest of my body. As my luck has it, the phone stops ringing just as I make it all the way to the bottom of the stairs. Conversation wouldn't come easily for me right now, anyway.

Thankful for the sleep-filled day, I decide to make a snack plate of cheese and apples and go to sit in the library. I curl my legs up beside me, feeling a little more myself and looking every bit like the lazy cat that should be curled up with me. However, I didn't hear her cry for food all day, nor did she lay with me in bed as I slept.

I call for her, waiting for her assured reply, but hear no pitter-patter of paws. Carya is always within a stone's throw away from me. This silence irks me.

I slip on my house shoes and check every door, hoping she didn't get locked in one of the estate's many rooms. No luck. But then I remember, there was one door that was left open for some of the evening last night.

The basement door is definitely closed when I approach it, while an anxious energy finds the center of my chest. Thoughts of Carya being locked in that dark, damp cold basement make guilt wiggle its way to the pit of my gut. I open the door and peer down the long, gloomy stairwell. A musty gust of air wraps around me as I peer into the cobweb-filled stairwell.

"Carya!" I yell, but nothing. "Carya!" Still nothing.

The basement's cold concrete walls swallow the echo I hoped to hear. I'm about to turn around, but that guilt tugs at my conscience, leaving me no choice but to take a step down hesitantly. It can't be that bad, thinking how I just did this last night. The only difference is now I'm on my own.

I make it to the bottom, and a flicker of something catches my eye toward the back. It must be Carya. I grab the candle sconce and light it, thankful that I forgot my Bic down here last night. Steadily, I make my way toward the back room that seems to go on forever.

My steps swoosh against the cold, hard floor in my thick, muted pink slipper socks. It is the only sound I hear, and it lingers in the air far longer than I'd like.

It gets colder as I get closer, and I wrap my arms around my shoulders. Partly to make myself warmer, and partly because I am terrified of what I'll find as I move toward the large entry. The same one that Que stole me away from uncovering last night.

I make my way to the frame of the room, but find no glimpse of Carya. Instead, what I find is even more perplexing. Two large wooden doors encased in earth and ivy buried within the back walls.

How ivy grows down in this dark abyss makes no sense, but I see it clear as day, deep and green. The doors are trunk-like, covered in dense, twisting roots—barely recognizable as doors at all. The only way to make out their shape is by the glow they emit from behind.

One holds a moonlight fuzz around it, flaring mixes of iridescent hues, while the other holds a deep blue-green glow that shines fiercely like the sea against the morning sun. I can almost feel the energy that each is emitting against my skin. Both feel completely different from one another as I place my hand against the rough bark of them. Both feel well known in a place deep down in my chest.

I work to tear some of the moss-covered roots off of the doors. Most of the roots fall away with ease, but there are some stubborn bits that refuse to budge beneath my ravage. The door with the green aura is home to the ones that are the most stubborn. I give up ripping out the resistant bits that remain and wipe my hands against my sweatpants.

My mind is swimming with what could be behind these doors. They could lead to another world for all I know. Or based on the sheer amount of alcohol in this place, perhaps they open up to an old hidden speakeasy.

Judging by how far I walked to reach them, I'm probably beneath the far side of the property. But why would the basement be that large? And how am I not swimming in water right now? Basements in this part of Louisiana are near impossible to exist, so why is this one here and thriving?

Que was right. This is a curious house, and this basement is the most perplexing of the lot. I lean in, putting my ear against the green glowing door, listening for a hint of something, anything. But all I can hear is the deep whirring of its energy. And while my ears find nothing, my fingers discover something instead.

I step back to inspect a tiny circular indentation carved into the wooden door. Someone placed a tiny stone within the circular groove. The same color stone that matches that of my mother's jade willow tree. Which means it also matches the ring I found within that broken tree that is now tucked away safely at the bottom of a drawer in my room upstairs. *The ring*, my mind echoes.

My eyes widen with realization. I all but race for the stairs, fumbling on my feet as I do, and make my way to the main stairwell that lead to my room. Finding the ring right where I knew it would be, I dash back to the basement and the two very eerie doors that wait for me. I have all but forgotten my nerves about this part of the house, feeling only desperate excitement at the discovery at hand.

I step closer to the green door. My fingers almost dropping the ring within the darkness of the basement floor. Somehow I keep it in my grasp, and stick the ring inside the round indent.

With the placement of the ring in the circle, the roots react, but not in the way I wish. They become thicker, longer, growing to encase the door even more. Whatever is within doesn't want me to discover it.

I also notice a new faint light around the door buzzing to be seen. The closer I look, I see there is an inscription framing the edges, but I cannot make out the language. I am well read, having to be so with all my work on antique history. But in all my research of places I have been, I have never seen a language written like this.

I look for a knob or anything I might turn to grab leverage on the door. A way to pry it open, but there is nothing. With the now thicker barricade around the green one, I do not know what steps to take next. The secret words continue to flicker like a curse.

I keep trying to look for another way in, but ultimately I am defeated. My excitement wanes to the lowest low. With reluctance, I walk back to the stairway, toying with the ring between my fingers, trying to wrap my head around the connection the ring has to the door and the strange glow it holds within.

Something on the ring pokes me, and I suck my breath inward in the form of a small gasp. I look closely at the ring, and notice something I had not before. The ring has tiny thorns inlaid in it.

They are so small. Unnoticeable at first glance, but that tiny prick was enough to let a minuscule drop of blood spill from my throbbing finger and land on the basement floor. Building in a strange luminescence of its own before vanishing into the concrete floor—a not-so-subtle hint of what my future here holds.

20

THE ARGUMENT

RACINE 1978

As down on my spirits as I was, I was utterly ravenous once coming up the stairs. After all that time in the basement, I realize I hadn't eaten today—the emptiness now roaring to be noticed. My snack plate left forgotten after looking for Carya, whom I still haven't found.

I devour leftovers from the night before and make my way to the library, but the soft meowing at the front door has me scrambling to open it. Carya bursts through the door at the first hint of an opening. My heart eases, so very relieved to see her.

I pick her up. Filthy is putting it kindly. Dirt and leaves cling to her orange fur. She hasn't been outside since we came here, being that I wasn't sure what animals live in the wild here, and I didn't want to risk it. So how she got outside, I have no idea.

She even has a faint smell of must and earth emanating from her slinky body, much like the basement I just came from. A cat this dirty should be bathed, but she must read my mind because she darts off before her feet even touch the tile.

The knock on the door is abrupt. Each event today is happening before I can collect myself from the one prior. Opening the door again, I find Ry pacing about on the other side. There is a fire in his eyes. An angry, all-consuming fire.

"Is everything alright, Ry?" I ask, getting annoyed that he hasn't been able to speak a word yet.

"I've tried calling," he bites out. "Where have you been? What is the use of a phone if you don't answer it?" I have little patience for men who think that people should be at their beck and call, so my annoyance grows.

"I've been here. Sleeping," I say. Trying to diffuse his agitation, I add, "Can you take a minute and just chill out, please? Your aggression is not necessary...like, *at* all."

Ry places his hands along the doorway above his head. He closes his eyes, taking a deep breath through his nose. I watch the angst coil out of his body. *Much better.*

It's darker out now, and as Ry stands there, I can smell the last bits of warm southern air surround us. Finally calming himself enough, Ry opens his eyes and meets my own.

"I'm sorry, Jade. I was worried, and then I felt...I thought something happened to you," Ry explains, as a more leveled man emerges.

"It's OK, but there are few places I could get into trouble around here. I know almost no one, so seriously, you shouldn't worry." I say reassuringly. And then with a tilt of my head, I lightly chuckle, "Although, you *did* say the trees themselves are dangerous. I guess they could always swallow me whole."

I tip the corner of my mouth up, thinking he'd be amused, but the look he shoots me makes it clear he is anything but. OK, no room for jokes today. The headache from earlier still lingers under my temple, making my tolerance for this man, who thinks he can project his illogical worry onto me, almost nonexistent. I try my hardest anyway.

"No, you don't get it, Jade. You make me feel things. Things I'd rather not," he confesses.

He makes his way through the door and closes it behind him. He is mere inches from me, and I can't help but place my hand on his chest, palming his racing heart in my hand. Whatever he has been going through over worrying about me, I can feel there.

I glance up into two eyes that are fierce with fear and angst. Ry tilts his head down and our foreheads meet in a soft understanding.

"Just please answer your phone from now on," he asks as a nervous plea.

"I'll do my best, sir." I can't object to his worrying, even if it's a little over the top. I reach my hand up and graze his jaw. The sharp shock that never stops every time I touch him, shoots down my hand and seeps into my being. I can feel his care and his relief that nothing has happened to me.

But something new lies there. Is it hunger, perhaps? A hunger that feels guarded. Too restrained. Building to a head like a predatory bird waiting for the right moment to swoop down to claw its prey.

Before I get too carried away with what I think he feels, I touch my lips to his. A sure way to alleviate this endless mind chatter with a single action. It works.

Ry's kiss is deep and pressing, like he wants more of me than I can give. It's discomforting. He grabs me closer, rougher, slamming me against the wall in his urgency. My head hitting with a thud. He is brasher than normal, but not unwelcome.

He must've bitten my lip—I taste metal as our tongues slide against each other. He grows even wilder once he tastes what I do, and he fists his hand around the band of my sweatpants, pulling them so tight I think they'll rip.

He releases them, his motions harsh and provoked. A hint of chaos wraps around me. Not the normal Ry I've gotten the last couple times we've put ourselves in this position.

Ry then grips my wrists with the same hand and holds them over my head. His mouth moving to my neck, and his length hardens against me as he presses the weight of himself onto me. I adjust my legs to welcome him, but he must need to know for sure.

His other hand dips beneath the band of my sweatpants, and he moves it lower and lower until he feels the pool of swollen arousal between my legs. Now it's clear. I want him.

He mimics an unleashed animal growling against my skin. And I feel what he has become. Something primal. I have been waiting to be unleashed with him again—even if he may eat me alive.

I rock against his fingers as he moves them closer to my core. One finger, then two. Just as I feel I may burst with the fullness inside, he squeezes in another, all while his mouth roams lower down my tank top and he licks my nipple through the fabric.

He is sucking and I am grinding myself on his fingers, which move in and out of me. My toes barely touch the floor as his hand still captures my wrists against the wall. Both of his hands being the only thing keeping me afloat. Suspended in his grasp is where I long to be most.

"I want you to come for me, my sweet succulent. I want you to make a mess of my fingers, so I can lick them clean." With those words accompanied by his warm breath against the peak of my wet, stiff nipple, I am lost.

I squirm against him, but he pins me so I can barely move, his fingers still curling in and out of me. I let out a scream of pleasure as he nibbles the small bud of my nipple, piercing through.

And as I come down from this thrill, my mind flashes. I see my blood spilling in the river over the bridge, my body hanging limply from a rope in a castle I've dreamt of before. My blood seeping into the roots of the large hickory. No, I will not let this moment be ruined. I focus again on my physical senses.

His mouth moves slowly back up to my neck as he lowers me down, and my body stands limp and tired from my release. I watch as he takes his fingers out of my sweats, bringing them to his blood-smeared mouth as he follows through on his threat.

"Open your mouth," he orders and pulls my hair so I'm looking straight up at the ceiling. The odd angle of my head causing my neck to ache as he pulls my hair harder still.

The collected lover by the fire? Gone. He looms over me with my mouth open, and without warning, spits what he just licked off his fingers of me into my mouth. He then loosely grabs me by the neck, using his thumb to nudge my jaw up and close my mouth.

"Swallow." I do. In this moment, I'm afraid of what will happen if I don't obey him. He scoops me up with one arm under my behind, tossing me over his shoulder, where he takes me upstairs to the bed and fully has his way with me.

As he does, the outside matches the bed we occupy. Wind rushes against the house, and the house talks back in groans and creaks. Branches from the nearby trees crawl along the white walls in shadow form, growing and stretching from the light of the moon.

I am left with many thoughts when he finishes. At times, I was close to telling him to stop, but the force felt warranted. And before I could say anything, I was lost to the pleasure again.

But this experience with him was different. That is certain. And what do I know of him truly? He has so much darkness clouding what's within. But I gave him no reason to think I wanted him to stop. And if this is nothing to him, he doesn't make it seem that way.

We barely know each other, although I feel as if he's been written deep in my soul long ago. His essence slowly melted into every fiber of my being. I'm not sure how, but a large part of me calls out to him as if it has been there all along.

"I found something odd in the basement today," is all I can seem to muster. He instantly sits up and looks at me like I told him the sky was falling, which seemed it actually may have while we were doing the deeds we just performed.

"What do you mean?" he demands, his voice making me timid. Again. I am not normally one to retreat when I am spoken to with the aggression he does, but it's as if an unknown memory makes me instinctively close up.

"There were these two doors. And...this may sound odd, but this ring I found the day I met you at my shop, it fits perfectly within a nook on one of the doors. It was as if it belonged there." I look to him, hoping I haven't scared him away with my confession. "...isn't that bizarre?"

"I told you not to go down there," he yells, and stands up harshly from the bed. His hostility bites, and I'm infuriated with how he thinks I need to obey him like I'm his. The man I adore has been nowhere in sight today. Only a controlling masochist seems to have taken his place.

"Last time I checked, this was my house. And what is your problem with the basement, anyway?" I find my voice, speaking with assurance.

"What happened down there? Where is the ring? I knew it; I felt it. Damn it, Jade," he continues as if he is doing nothing wrong. "You don't understand the danger that awaits you in that basement. I've been trying to keep you away for a reason. I need us to have one life that isn't torn apart by this damned promise..." What does he mean by promise? And how can he think this is an acceptable way to speak to me?

"Well, nothing happened anyway," I say, trying to stay calm and be the steadier one. "When I put the ring near the doors, these roots seemed to grow. It was like a reaction to it or something—like a barricade. I put the ring back in my desk after it poked me."

The last comment breaks whatever composure he had left.

"What do you mean it poked you?! You bled? Fuck!" He all but screams the last word. He grabs my hands, but I pull them away. I can no longer enable this type of treatment.

"What is wrong with you? Why are you so angry?" I ask, holding in my tears, putting more and more space between us.

"I need to know if it made you bleed, Jade. Tell me now!" He's frantic with his words, and his hands grasp at my shoulders. I can't pull away this time. Tears well up in my eyes, and it's all I can do not to let them fall.

"The tiniest bit, but I'm fine," I barely choke out. "It was just a prick."

"You are so far from OK, Jade. This explains so much. I cannot save you now." I don't like the way he is saying my name. Full of anger and hunger, like he wants to be the one to make me bleed.

His eyes change then. And I watch his scars rise before my eyes, but he gets out of the bed to look out the window before I can see what they become. The tension spilling from him is so thick I could cut it with a knife. And I can't be sure I saw what I did, but before he turned, it looked as if those scars were forming into branches.

I'm not sure what terrifies me more—the thought I'm losing my mind, or the man standing in front of me.

"I need...I need a minute. I am going to start a bath," I say to him, tears actively running down my cheeks. I find my will to stand up, my shaky hands wrapping a floral sheet around my naked body. "I think it's best if you are gone by the time I come out of the bathroom."

He says nothing, but I know he will be gone, because how can one stay after a moment like that? I ask one more thing.

"And I'm a grown woman. Who on earth do you need to save me from?" It's more of a rhetorical question. One I don't expect him to answer. His voice does come, though. It's not until I've closed the bathroom door, but I hear him clearly.

"From me."

21

THE REUNION
RACINE 1978

Two weeks pass. I haven't heard from Ry since our confrontation the other night, nor do I want to. While I've struggled with the possibility of never seeing him again, I think it is for the best. A little lie that I tell myself to keep from crumbling apart.

My only saving grace has been taking walks around the property and falling in love with every tree nook, every aroma coming from a mix of the bayou and the forest surrounding it, and every piece of cascading garland of Spanish moss above me.

I can see why my uncle never wanted to leave. It's hard to find any other place as magical as this. It's late October now, marking my three-month point of being down here. Safe to say I love it more every day.

I've been getting a couple of rooms ready for Ashton and Lollie. It seems more urgent than ever to have their peaceful presence near. I've been checking all the boxes and prepping the spare rooms with a diligent efficiency. They both arrive together today, and the excitement within is helping me power through this day.

I can only imagine the amount of bickering and snide remarks that fills their car ride. I'm sure Lollie will all but jump out of the car when she gets here. Those two in small quarters for a twenty-hour drive, the Gods bless them both.

While I wait, I put some soup on and travel to the old willow tree, who always welcomes me by the sway of her boughs as I walk closer. I never feel more at home than when I am here in the presence of this majestic tree. Not even my mother's shop in Detroit can conjure this feeling of belonging.

That's because I am here, my love.

It is but a whisper in my ear. In some otherworldly dimension, I know it is my mother. I wrap the light sweater around my arms. Although it doesn't get cold here like it does in Detroit, I still feel a slight breeze. Winds of change heralding a message that it is still peak hurricane season.

I am grateful I found some old sweaters among the boxes. Even *they* feel like my mother. Everything reminds me of her, which must be why I hallucinated her hushed uttering.

The past two weeks have increased my visions of her as well as others that aren't as reassuring. In one more recent vision, everyone I knew morphed into trees. And when I traveled below their roots, whole worlds existed below. Worlds fueled by my blood. I think my mind took that old book about the realms below the trees a little too seriously.

My mind wanders to Ry, still so bothered by the way he reacted. Even more so, I am bothered by the part of me that still longs for his touch. I even long for the roughness that he brought the last time I saw him. It's like no matter how toxic his traits are, they are a toxin I wouldn't mind ingesting. I want him close, and I'm afraid what that says about me.

The smell of him surrounds me then, and I look toward the direction of the old hickory. It is rather far, but I can still see its highest branches. I've had terrible nightmares about it since our fight. Nightmares that leave me wondering how this man could remind me so much of my favorite tree.

The vile aggression I got to see firsthand, and I can't help but wonder if that is the real him. But aren't we all just varying shades of dark and light? Part yin and part yang. Part branches reaching for the light of the sun as well as roots burrowing deeper to reach the darkness below the surface. Both equally necessary to grow.

I am about to be lured that way when I hear the crunching of wheels on the driveway. I smile right away knowing who is here, all but running. Lollie's car comes into view. She waves her hands in delight.

It's been too long since I've seen them, and I am overjoyed with the pleasure seeing them evokes. The car stops, and as expected, Lollie all but leaps from it's open door. My feet move of their own accord, making my way to my best friends.

"Lol!" I yell in happiness, and we clutch each other like our lives depend on it.

"Oh. My. God, Jade! I have missed you so much. And look at you! Wow, maybe there is something to this Louisiana air because you look positively radiant!" Lollie gushes.

Ashton climbs out, approaching our over-the-top reunion like it's a wildlife documentary, nonchalantly tossing the keys up in front of him. He may be trying to hide how thrilled he is, but the grin he is holding back is a dead giveaway.

"She's not wrong, Jade. You look great." Ashton says in a genuine but cautious manner. Like an older brother who can't quite believe I am doing well here on my own.

I make my way over to him. We both lean into a much-needed embrace. My two greatest friends at my new favorite destination. Nothing could be better.

"I am so glad you guys are here. How was the car ride?" I look between the two of them. They look at each other, and I think I notice a faint blush from Lollie, but then she puts her hands to her throat in a choking pose, dramatizing how she felt about the long journey. There she is. I try to hold back my amusement for Ashton's sake.

"Fine," Ashton shrugs like no big deal.

"Yeah, no, it was fine. Buuuut what's not fine is how starving I am. Please tell me you have food here, Jade?" Lollie looks at me in her 'I need food now' type of look. I wink at her, because not only is there warm soup on the stove, but I stocked the pantry with all her favorite snacks knowing how much she needs to eat.

"Follow me," I say. Right away Lollie is clearly speechless, her jaw to the floor.

"No fucking way. This is all yours?" She exclaims, thrill taking over as she spins around the foyer, taking it all in. She surprisingly fits right into the vibe of this house.

I can't help but smile at her as I move them toward the kitchen and quickly put some soup into the brown vintage crock bowls I found hidden deep within the cupboards. We settle down around the countertop ready to have a major catch-up session.

Ashton, who is not much for words anyways, looks around and spots the basement door. He eyes it nervously and looks to Lollie, who is fully immersed in the minestrone soup in front of her. Something has changed between these two. Maybe the drive gave them a chance to have the heart to heart they so desperately needed.

When we are down to the last spoonful in our bowls, I go on to tell them they have their choice of six bedrooms. There are three downstairs and three upstairs, each having its own unique style. Either my uncle had a very varied decorating palette, or there were multiple people living here at one point. Oddly enough, they both choose bedrooms on the bottom floor—directly across from each other.

Once Lollie is settled in her room, she comes up to mine, wanting to know all about my stay here thus far. In-depth details about what has transpired between me and Ry sit at the tip of my tongue, but thankfully I manage to keep them there. As well as any mentions of Cher and Que.

I'm not sure why I don't divulge my new acquaintances to Lollie. I've always told her every aspect of my life, but I'm halted whenever I'm about to spill their names. Maybe it's because Lollie has always been a bit of a jealous type. It has always been just she and I.

"So, you two were seeing a lot of each other, huh?" She continues to pry. In any normal situation I would tell her, but something about what Ry and I shared seems so intimate and I'd like to keep it that way.

"We were, but merely to talk business. He helped out a lot when I first came here. I haven't seen him much lately, though. Oh, I found this really cool record shop. I have to take you there while you're here!" I add in trying to divert the topic, and it works.

We talk more about my doings with the house and property, and she catches me up on the shop, which sounds like it is doing the same as when I left.

"Everything alright between you and Ash?" I flat out ask, knowing I am coming on a little strong. Something Lollie isn't used to from me. Maybe this place has already changed me more than I know.

"Of course, why wouldn't it be?" She says through a blush.

"I don't know. You two just haven't been bickering as much. I thought for sure that car ride would do you both in." I tell her, and I think she is about to say something, but Ashton knocks at the door.

We both spin our heads around like we're in middle school, and have been caught smoking cloves behind the gym. True story, by the way, and also how that little habit of mine started.

"Hey, Ash!" I say and try to act like we weren't just talking about him.

"Hey," he says, and eyes Lollie. "Are you guys ready to go explore the town?"

"Oh, is that plan, then? I see you don't waste any time," I say and jump up from the bed. "Let me get my coat!"

I leave the two of them to continue whatever weird vibe they are sending each other, and they take some time before meeting me downstairs. When they finally do, I don't miss the subtle glimpse they make toward each other.

To ease this awkward exchange, I ask Ashton how his shop is doing, warmly missing the other shop people on our street. Our street is like a family. All the shop owners look out for each other. So, I listen intently as we load up into the car.

He tells me it's been slower now that it's gotten colder for fall. Michigan weather is always tricky as you never know what you are going to get. Snow and wind don't bode well even for the most popular shops in our city. But besides that, he tells me everyone is doing great. Comforting knowledge for the place I used to call home.

Ashton's car takes the drive with ease, then the topic flips yet again to what I've been hoping to avoid. The people I've met here. I've been here three months, so I guess it would be odd if I didn't make at least one new friend.

I reveal little, still straying from the names that send an uncertain panic through my system. But I do tell them about the kind restaurant owners, Walt and Cattie. The only interaction I've had with them has been through their restaurant, and *mostly* positive.

"Can we meet them?" Ashton asks. I can't be sure that intermingling these two worlds together is a good idea. Everyone I've met here comes with secrecy wrapped in a bow. I take pride in protecting the two people I love most on this planet by keeping those bows tied up tightly.

"We probably *should* go eat there. You both will fall in love with their menu." I say, hoping I can get lucky enough that the owners won't be there when we do. I would dread for them to bring up Ry, or mention something that sparks too many questions.

The main part of town comes into focus, and I make an impromptu and illogical decision to introduce them to Cher's shop. If she is there, she seems the least likely to cause any lasting damage. I just really want to share with them my favorite discovery in this small bayou town that she just happens to own.

So, I park on the little side street near a section of old townhouse shops. The brick road is unsteady under our feet as we all make our way into the dark brick building where Cher works, which is also the record store of my dreams. This is *totally a* good idea.

Stepping into this nostalgic portal makes me immediately giddy, but both Ashton and Lollie are looking toward the back of the shop. Instead of rummaging through the records right away, they seem more focused on the man who sits in the far chair placed in the corner of the store, eyes closed with his arms above his head. Que.

I should have known. Looking as if he owns this place even when he appears in his own world. Or I think he seems in his own world, but I watch as he peeks one eye open—aimed right at me. With a tilt of his mouth, he opens both eyes and leans forward in the chair, clasping his hands between his knees. A come-hither disposition that has me wanting to do just that.

Eyes locked, we stare a little too long. Lollie clears her throat, sparking my attention away from the devilish man and back to the reality of where we are and who I'm here with.

"So, you've left this one out of your list of new acquaintances, I see." She is looking at me with one eyebrow raised and a very know-ing, amused look gracing her petite pixie face.

He is beautiful. I can admit that. Anyone who has two eyes can see that, but there is something else that pulls me toward him. One would think it would be carnal in nature—it is not. It is an intimate understanding. Every time I look at him, I can relate. But to what? I don't know.

While Lollie seems intrigued with my reaction to this man, Ashton just stares daggers. If Que can feel this, he doesn't let on. He stands up and stretches his back, as if he is in no hurry. I watch as a sliver of his midriff becomes exposed in his black shirt and fitted jacket. Looking away proves challenging, which Lollie notices.

I dart my eyes away, flipping them at her. Like she doesn't drool at men who look like him on a regular basis. But not many look like him. In fact, as I think about this, I find it odd that she doesn't seem the least bit interested. The Lollie I know would have already introduced herself to a man like that as well as wiggled her way into his nightly itinerary.

Que strolls toward Ashton, all the while his eyes glued to me. When he directs his attention to Ashton, he holds his hand out. A challenge Ashton accepts. A dual of wills on who will be the first to break their handshakes.

"Hello, you must be Jade's best friends from Detroit. I'm Que." Que directs his comment Ashton's way. They both stare at each other. Not saying much with words, but they don't need to. Finally, they let go of each other's hands, and the standoff thankfully ends.

"I'm Ashton, and this is Lollie," Ashton says, breaking the silence. The tension still buzzing in intensity.

"Hello, Que." Lollie says with a tilt of the head. "It seems you've heard about us, but I can't say we've heard about you." And it is in that moment that I try to think back on the times I have talked about Ashton and Lollie to anyone here. Of those moments, I don't recall being with Que at all. I must have mentioned them the other night when we were drinking wine, and maybe that is why I can't seem to remember.

"That's probably for the best," Que says, in a deep tone that rattles my senses. And with that comment, he walks past us and out the door. Not even a glance back in our direction.

"Well, I can see why you didn't mention him. I would hope to forget that kind of smug attitude too if I were you," Ashton comments, exposing his annoyance at the whole interaction.

"He's just really intense, but I barely know him," I rush my words. "He came over for dinner just the once, and kind of uninvited at that." I realize my mistake then, when they both snap their heads to look at me. My unfiltered mouth gets the very best of me.

"What!?" They exclaim, as if it's a big deal. But things have changed in the last few months here. *I've* changed. Gone is the tame, calculated girl they knew back in Detroit.

"Oh yeah, I had Cher over, and she kind of brought him along. Just a harmless dinner. The company was a pleasant change since coming here. I don't know many people yet." I add while browsing one of the record crates on the table against the wall, hoping to make the entire dinner event seem more casual than it actually was. Especially between Que and me.

"Nothing about him says harmless," Lollie says with eyes that say more. She isn't wrong. "And who is this friend? I haven't heard about this harmless man or this new friend until now. Wish you would've let me in on that information, Jade." Lollie's wariness shining through.

"I just met them, actually, so there has been little to tell. I had them over for dinner once, and that was it. But it was nice." I say honestly. I look to Lollie, who I can tell is bummed it took so long for me to tell her about the people I've met here, but she smiles as she always does.

We both pull each other in for a hug. A habit we have always done when we've reached a mutual understanding after miscommunication. Lollie and I always bounce back. That's just how we're built.

Ashton is a different story. He's been quiet. Too quiet. He is super protective of me, always has been since he moved across from Moon Shadow Collectibles all those years ago. He was just a young man himself, helping his dad stock the local food market shop.

When he is this quiet, it puts me on edge. Watching me while chewing his bottom lip deep in thought, I can tell he doesn't know what to think of this whole situation. The truth is, neither do I, but that's on me to figure out.

"Who is the new friend then?" He asks, and since he had already met the one person I was hoping they would not, I figure there is no harm in telling them now. She seems nice enough.

"Her name is Cher. She's super friendly, and well, this is her shop." And as if she heard us call her name, Cher appears from behind the back shop door, coffee in hand and a smile on her cheerful face. She spots us and makes her way over. There is no way to ease them into her now.

"Jade!" She says brightly, and pulls me into an embrace whether I wanted one or not. "How are you? I'm still nursing a hangover from dinner the other night, believe it or not. Please tell me you fared better than I did?" She asks and slowly looks around at Lollie and Ashton, who have stepped closer to me at this point. "Oh my, you have company. So sorry to invade. I am Cher!" she says in a way that gives no hint of her actually being sorry.

"Hi, Cher. This is Ashton and Lollie. Two of my dearest friends from Detroit," I announce. This introduction being a lot more welcome than the last. Or at least I think it is. I notice Lollie has a stoic look on her face the whole time, like she will not let her guard down. Odd behavior for someone who befriends literally everyone she meets.

Cher invites us all out to dinner tonight, not caring about my friends' reception of her. Both Ashton and Lollie agree to join with a bit of reluctance. After all, they've been dying to see everything about the town I've been calling my residence for the last few months. We all settle on meeting Cher at Tallulah's Cajun Bar later tonight, and then promptly leave the scene of more than *one* rather awkward encounter today.

The comfortable October air makes it ideal to walk to *The*

Spanish Moss, our destination for brunch. I am lucky enough that the owners are nowhere in sight, and as I had predicted, Lollie and Ashton ate their way through tomorrow, leaving just enough time to check out more of the town. We drag a reluctant Ashton around, popping in and out of as many shops as we can for most of the afternoon, until he finally asks if we can spare him by going home.

"I need a nap if I plan to make it out tonight with you girls. We weren't all born with loads of energy that allows us to look aimlessly at worthless trinkets all day." He jokes, obviously referring to Lollie. She doesn't miss a beat.

"Oh, don't we know it, Grandpa." She says back and bats her eyelashes in his direction. His expression heats.

Their constant backhanded remarks are normal expectations in their strained relationship. However, there is something that isn't being said, and I've noticed strange subtleties between them since arriving here. Ashton is right, though. A small nap does sound rather nice.

———

Back at the estate, we all agree to go to our separate bedrooms. A welcome invitation of the rest our legs are begging for. I grab Carya, who is wandering the hall, scooping her warm frame up in my arms, and head to my room.

I make a quick go of taking off my brown suede skirt and throw on the sweats already bunched up on the end of my bed from this morning. Carya and I settle in, and I close my eyes, thinking how hard it will be to fall asleep with the excitement of my friends finally being here.

That doesn't last long, because I'm soon pulled into a dream. A dream connecting a daydream that swam through my mind mere weeks ago when standing on the exact bridge.

I am running to the river toward a stone bridge mounted up high.

The bridge sits in anticipation, as if waiting for footfalls to be heard against its hardened trail.

I feel something wet against my face. There is no rain. I touch my face, and my hand comes away damp. Tears. I don't know why or for whom, but I'm crying.

I brace myself at the railing of the bridge, finding my shoes grasping at the rounded stones to raise myself up to the top of the ledge. I look down, knowing this river will surely pull me in at first contact with the muddy water, but I don't think it will do what I want without some help.

I hear movement on the bridge and look to my left. A man is running toward me; screaming, but his face is blank. It all comes back to me.

It's always him. Over and over, wrecking my heart like it means nothing. If I live anymore in this world knowing what I know and seeing what I've seen of love or lack thereof, I will slowly lose both my soul and my mind.

One is not meant to know these things, and that is why I jump. But before I do, to make sure it is a death that sticks. I take a small blade from my dress pocket and move it deep into each of my wrists. It doesn't hurt. Nothing could hurt as much as my heart does at this moment, knowing all that I do. And that is all I remember, because I know that is where my life ended.

I wake a hot mess of sweat. My heart beating through my chest. I have never had a dream like that. It felt so real. A forgotten memory —impossible, since the me in that dream never made it out alive.

One detail stands out, though. As the blade made its way into each wrist, my mind's eye caught a glimpse of something familiar on my ring finger. A ring that sits alone in a box on my dresser drawer, just inches away from where I lay in bed now.

22

NEW AND OLD FRIENDS

RACINE 1978

Old feelings of bubbly girlhood rush back with the way Lollie is dolling me up, reminiscent of being back home. Ashton is pacing by the door, already ready to go. Why are some men always in such a hurry? It's as if they think time will explode if their needs aren't met within the instant of them developing.

I watch Ashton pace back and forth and Lollie, slowly pinning up my hair as if she doesn't have a care in the world. A sentiment we share for the time being until I realize she is doing this on purpose, making him anxiously wait for us out of spite.

The games between these two are next level since their arrival here. It's always been tense between them, but never like this. I decide to take matters into my own hands.

"Alright, I think I look good enough, Lol," I say with a start and sit up from the small wood vanity, brushing the wrinkles out of my dark green mini dress.

Some of the long bangs that Lollie just pinned back in a half-do messily fall back around my face. I don't miss Lollie tipping her eyes to the ceiling and then looking at Ashton. He sends an equally annoyed grin her way.

These two know the best way possible to get under each other's skin. If I didn't know how much they fluster each other, I would think they were secretly getting together behind closed doors. I cannot imagine that happening, with their history.

With a nudge in the right direction, I manage to keep them from killing each other and get them out the door.

———

The bar is a vibe. Its atmosphere pulses with music and sweat and something that feels like enchantment. The air flows freely, full of trumpets and sax blaring a bluesy song, along with its patrons swaying to the sensual tune.

Lollie and I don't miss a beat and head straight to the bar. The giggles still have the best of us, and we take a few shots before making our way to the table Ashton saved for us. This is the bar we said we would meet Cher in, but I have yet to spot her amongst the crowd.

Lollie has to all but scream at me on top of the music. It's so different from our bars back in Detroit. No underlying melancholy hidden within hazy plumes of cigarette smoke. No, this place feels like a million shooting stars landed in this room and radiated their magic into every musician, bartender, and occupant. Alive is how I feel, and also right at home.

I watch as Lollie slides a drink to Ashton, and he takes it. The man who never drinks. Good. It'll be nice to see him let loose a bit. Although, knowing him, it'll be one drink and back to playing body-guard, but I'm grateful for his strait-laced way. And Lollie. Bringing me a calm comfort in this tumultuous sea of new.

We are about one drink in when I notice a shift in the air, and I catch sight of Que at the bar. It's hard not to miss him, so I wonder how long he has been there. He has a drink in his hand and must feel my studying eyes. He turns his head slightly, his eyes meeting mine.

Before, in the basement, there was vulnerability there. That's not what lies within them now. He is calculating in the way he looks at me. He winks, and from where I sit in the pink velvet booth, I swear I see his iris catch moonlight like a mirror.

Cher walks up beside him and finds where his glance lingers. Immediately she smiles and makes her way to our table.

"There you are! I hope you weren't waiting long. Que was a pain to drag out here." She says as she shimmies her way in to sit beside me.

I look to Que, who is now back to gazing into his drink at the bar, and I wonder how they are even friends. So completely opposite. But then, I guess so are Lollie and I. What is that saying they say about opposites?

Speaking of Lollie, her face is cool and collected, which may look fine to an outsider, but I know her. I can tell she is not thrilled with the fact that Cher actually showed up on the night out she invited us to.

"Oh, not a problem! We've just been enjoying this bar. It's so..." I say trying to describe it.

"It's a lot, I know. It's one of the lesser-known old-time bars. Faces around here can get too familiar for Que and me. I bet your friend, tall, dark and handsome, would say the same. He's lived here about as long as Que, but they stay on separate paths. Just as you rarely see a hawk frolicking with crows," Cher says cryptically, but it's a comment that resonates.

It's the first time I have really thought about Ry since Ashton and Lollie showed up. It sends a swirl to my stomach, which surprises me. I have been doing a good job of keeping him off my mind since our argument. As far as I can tell, he has done the same with me.

"Yeah, what's the deal with those two? Do they know each other?" I ask Cher, and Lollie scoots closer to me. I then realize my slip of bringing up Ry with Lollie here, but it's too late to take it back now. Lollie sends me a concerned look, feeling more and more kept in the dark.

"They do. Once upon a time, they had been close friends. But, as it does with most friends turned to enemies, love came between them. Love and other emotions of sorts. Now, it seems they are *rooted* here, so to speak," Cher says in a way that leaves a lot to the imagination. "She was a pretty one, though. Fun, too. Actually, she reminds me a lot of you..." she says with a twist. Her words send a troublesome chill down my spine.

She glances toward my two friends with a smile that doesn't meet her eyes. Lollie is not impressed, her icy stare boring into Cher. When Lollie notices me watching, she darts her eyes away.

"OK, who are we talking about?" Lollie asks, now acting confused, looking between me and Cher. "I am definitely missing parts of this story. Did you meet someone else, Jade, that I haven't been told about?" Lollie's hurt expression makes the guilt of holding information creep up on me.

"Uh, kind of. Just the man who came up to tell me about this place. Ry. The one I told you about, who had helped me clean up the property. I haven't seen him for months now," I lie.

It hurts to do so, and I don't even know why I do, because Lollie can tell. She looks at Ashton passing each other a worried glance, her lips forming a grimaced and strained expression.

"Well, thanks for keeping me and Ash in the loop," she utters. I can tell I've put her in a sour mood.

"Oh, Lol..." I say, but she just shrugs.

"Oh shoot, did I bring up something I shouldn't have?" Cher says and looks at Lollie. Cher sounds innocent enough, but I can see Lollie's jaw tighten. "Don't worry, Ry usually stays in his own little realm most days. You two probably won't even meet him." Cher adds as a final touch.

"It's fine, just...I don't know. Let's drink." Lollie says in her shut it down way when she is around people she is not completely comfortable talking to.

So, we do just that, even if it means we will have to address the topic later. We drink. We dance. I steal glances at Que, and he has stolen more than a few at me.

Thoughts of Ry bubble up. A guilty nagging sensation in my gut I can't ignore. I gave him the cold shoulder, but something internally tells me I should give in to his ways. I can't get him out of my head now.

Something felt so concrete when he was near. A tether to our souls that I could hold on to. I don't feel that with Que, but he *is* quite pleasant to look at.

It isn't long before Que finds his way closer. Easing his way behind me on the dance floor, but the intimacy feels wrong. I let him put his hands on my waist. There is no harm in dancing, but I want to see his face.

I spin around and wrap my arms around his neck. I'm reminded of one of my dreams, then. One where I am dancing with this very man. I know it. The smell of moonflowers surrounds us. The same smell as outside the Detroit dive bar, months back.

"Have I met you before?" I ask, feeling sure now.

"It's possible," Que says. "But it was way before you even knew." He pulls me closer, aware of where my body touches his. Oh, maybe this doesn't feel so wrong after all.

"What do you mean by that?" I'm curious now, Que having a way of engaging my mind in a way Ry does not.

"I've tried telling you this story before, but it didn't go so well. I don't think it's mine to reveal, little gem." For the faintest second, I think I know what he is talking about, but blank memories cloud it.

"I'm afraid I've only ever met you in my dreams, and even then, at a distance," is all I can think to say back. But it's the truth. I have seen him. Detroit. In my sleep. All imagined, I convince myself.

He darkens then, as if remembering the saddest story.

"It's a shame you weren't created for me. We could have been something real." His voice is low and aching. He kisses my head and leaves me there. Still and surprised, surrounded by dancing locals.

I walk away with my head down, hoping Lollie didn't see any of our interaction. The dance floor, with an array of geometric designs below my feet, makes my head slightly dizzy. Music is blaring in my ears, washing away a memory that begs to be revealed. None of the songs are familiar, but they seem to know me—and I let them.

I find our table and realize Lollie and Ashton are gone. A moment to observe that I find enduring. I've always been a people watcher, even as a child. My mother scolded the younger me for staring more times than I can count.

I felt a searching within me, looking for someone. That same feeling would cross me when I looked out at the estate and focused my eyes on the hickory tree. But there are no trees here, only drunken dancing and hearty sax.

I catch Cher talking with Que by the bar stool he reclaimed after leaving me stranded. They look to be arguing about something, but when she spots me watching, her entire demeanor changes. My staring was never one to go unnoticed.

She smiles and comes to sit down with me.

"So, Que and I are going to head out. But I wanted to tell you, I'm so happy you guys showed up. I don't know what you plan to do with your estate. But for selfish reasons, I feel you belong here." She stares at me intently, hoping I understand. I find her choice of words to hit me right where I need them to.

"It's seriously so nice to have a girl on my level here. I think even Que likes that you've come." I tilt my head at her reference to him. "Whatever choice you make, I hope you keep that in mind. Just know it's your choice to make," she states. And with that statement, she kisses me on the cheek and walks away.

It was the first spark of real, genuine conversation Cher has had with me, and I couldn't help but feel her words held a double meaning. Every word whispered to me this evening claws at me, like a subtle but urgent message from beyond this time.

I continue to watch Que. I can't help it. He is mesmerizing. His movements are swift and cocky, like everything he does is a game he must win without a care. A mask.

He responds to my stare with a quick salute after he downs his drink. I smile at him. I don't think it would hurt to get to know him better, not like it hurt with his old ex-friend.

After what Cher said, I can't help but wonder what choice I am going to make. Should I stay and find out what more this place has to offer? Or do I go back to my comfortable and predictable shop life back in Detroit?

As I'm in my head, Lollie shows up, her hair a bit disheveled. My eyes widen in amusement as I notice the lipstick smeared from her bee-stung lips.

"OK, I was going to ask *where* you've been, but from the looks of you, I think I need to ask with *whom* you've been." I say and look up at her, barely containing the laugh that is working its way up my throat. She laughs too, but uncomfortably.

"That obvious, huh?" she whispers.

"Completely," I respond exaggeratedly.

"And leave it to you to use proper English when you are drunk." She smiles then and adds, "Let's head home. Ashton is bringing the car around...at least I thought I saw him with the car keys heading outside." Lollie says quickly, looking away from me as she does.

"That's fine, but who is the mystery man?" I say, nudging her shoulder. She looks up, then down nervously, shaking her head in refusal.

"Honestly, I'd rather forget. Just a random who was getting way too handsy. So, like seriously, let's get out of here before he comes back." She says in a hushed voice.

We make our way outside; the warm air has faded with the sun. Just as Lollie mentioned, Ashton has the car pulled up and is waiting for us to hop in.

In the car, I realize I am actually a bit drunk and press my fingers between my eyes, trying my hardest not to get sick. Car rides and alcohol never mix well for me, and I try to distract myself from the ever-present spins by talking to Lollie.

"Remember when my mom would take us on random car trips out of the city? She'd just keep going until there were trees for miles," I say. Lollie looks at me. Her smile speaks of her remembering. "She loved the woods," I mumble out, realizing I'm slurring and possibly tearing up. But it feels good to talk about my mom. It's something I don't do enough.

"It was like she couldn't breathe until we were near nature or a pond or any body of water for that matter." Lollie reminisces with me, a sad smile tugging at her lips.

"And where there was water, there were willows. I loved how she would always make us take off our shoes and socks to dip our feet in. No matter what season," I reminisce. I'm full-on crying now, silently. Lollie's somber look beside me, telling me she is trying to hold herself together as well.

"There's a willow on the property. Remind me to show you tomorrow," I try to articulate through tears.

My heart sinks in the process, because I forgot they are taking off tomorrow. Then, I really start crying. And on cue, Lollie does, too.

"We didn't get enough time together. I don't want to leave you here," Lollie says through tears. She is quiet for a bit and then adds, "And...I don't trust those two. Cher seems off." I see Ashton, who's been quietly driving while letting us do our emotional dumping in the back seat. He gives her a look she returns in the driver mirror. He stays quiet.

"Look, Ash and I were talking, and we just think you should be careful. Those two seem weird. How well do you really know them? What if they are scammers? I could see that..." Lollie rambles.

"They are super nice. For real, Lol. Or at least Cher is. I promise." I say, trying to sound reassuring. But *do* I really know them?

"It's always the nice ones." Lollie looks at me, just saying anything to get through to me, but I refuse to let her get to me this time.

My whole life, I've been letting my mother and these two talk me out of decisions using fear. Their way of keeping me safe and close, but I never realized until coming here that I haven't really lived.

"Just watch out down here, Jade. I get a bad feeling." Ashton's voice is serious. And I may be too drunk to remember, but he continues, "Don't get too tangled up with any of these characters in this town. I don't trust them. Especially this Que guy." He looks at me, like I should see what he does.

"You guys are too much. But I'll gladly stay away from Que if it helps you all feel better." I say as we pull into the drive, hitting slight bumps that toss me off balance. Then I add, "This place is actually really interesting. I feel you guys barely touched the surface. There is so much history. And," and here comes the point when I should stop, but something compels me to continue, "the basement of this house is something else, you guys. There are these doors set into the walls..."

"How is there even a working basement here, Jade? Isn't Louisiana well below sea level? Sounds dangerous," Ashton chimes in, trying to invoke fear yet again, but I'm not done divulging these secrets that should stay just that.

"I found this ring too, and they seem to fit together. And get this. It's a jade ring, like what are the chances?" I know I'm going off on a tangent, but this is the first time the thoughts in my head have gotten the best of me. Thank you, alcohol.

I look up at them, but they don't seem as excited as I am. In fact, they look worried.

"Where's this ring?" Ashton asks in a concerned, not at all amused tone. Lollie sits quietly in the back seat next to me, wringing her hands together, looking between me and Ashton. Honestly, these two are acting stranger than anyone else here—which is saying something.

"It's in the house in a drawer," I answer, confused by their response. This isn't the first time someone has had this strong of a reaction to this ring.

Finding it by accident, but having it frequent my dreams and flood the circumstances of my newly gained estate, makes one wonder of its true origin.

"Show us," Lollie says in a way that makes her sound unsure if she really wants to see. I decide to do just that, hoping it'll bring me some much-needed answers as to why they are acting this way.

Once we make it to the house, I pull out the box and open it, but there is no ring in sight. Two empty spots greet me instead of just the one. The first missing one having no pull on my affliction. Probably long lost in the crack of a floorboard or amongst the grass on the property. Losing a ring like that would feel horrible, and now I know that feeling.

The beautiful ring that once drew my blood is missing. I rummage through the drawer, looking under papers and other odds and ends that were left there, but it is gone. And the looks on Ashton and Lollie's faces that were once strained—calm. Their shoulders relax as if I just undetonated a bomb in my hands. Our reactions being so opposite.

"So, you lost it, huh?" Ashton says, seeming a little calmer than he was in the car when I first told them about the ring.

"Yeah, I had it just a couple of days ago. Damn. It was so beautiful, you guys. The metal was a bit broken or something odd with the design. It cut me actually. I was going to take it to get fixed. But you should see this door...it matches it perfectly." I'm babbling again.

"It cut you?" Lollie whispers. She looks white as a ghost. "So, you put it on then?" She stares at me with an intensity as if she is questioning things I know.

"No, but I was in the basement." I explain. "It wasn't a big deal, just a drop. It wasn't rusty or anything. It's a quality ring. But did you hear me? You must see this door..."

"No!" Ashton surprises me with his reaction. "I'm just going to say it straight out. I don't like it here. This place is full of bad juju," Ash blurts out. "Jade, I think you need to come home. This house. It's nice, but it's not your home. The basement—it's old. Probably full of asbestos or mold. The air quality alone is reason enough to leave," Ashton says, reaching for anything.

Is he out of his mind? I'm starting to think everyone here has gone mad. He is the second person to tell me not to go into the basement.

"I don't understand. Seriously, what is up with you guys? It's just a ring. It's just a basement. It is just a house," I stammer, so confused with how my friends are acting.

"Jade, we just miss you. You belong with us back in Detroit. Here is..." Lollie starts to say something, but she stops. I can tell from their energy that they have something else to say.

"Look, it's been a long night. We are all tired. Let's just leave this where it is and know that we just want you to be careful. This place is strange, and its strangeness seems to affect everyone around here." Ashton's face says it all. "Just promise us you'll be careful. *Please.*" Ashton pleads.

"I will. I promise," I say. And I feel in my bones it's a fickle promise, because if they are right about one thing, it's that this place *is* quite strange, but I welcome it.

23
LOCAL BAR
RACINE 1978

Ashton and Lollie left days ago. Our heated discussion making their departure that much more bittersweet. They called to let me know they made it back to Detroit safely. Lollie said it was much more bearable having Ashton follow her as opposed to him driving and taking control over every aspect of her car. Regardless, it grounds me in the fact that they are hundreds of miles away.

The day they left, I sat around with my thoughts, petting Carya, and trying to figure out where I could have dropped the ring. I want to go in the basement, but Ashton actually scared me a bit with the thought of the air quality. Leave it to him to know just where to strike up my worry bone.

At this point, I am antsy, feeling locked up and secluded. A coil forms its way around my spine, edging me to release what I know lies beneath its tension. I still haven't talked to Ry, but he is a constant in my mind. The more I try to push thoughts of him away, the more I find my need grows.

The clock strikes seven pm with no sign my racing thoughts will die down anytime soon. I can't shake the way my friends acted by pointing out the strange flaws of this house. Their worry leaves me crawling in my skin, and I feel like I need to get out. Be somewhere to clear my head. Anywhere but in this house.

Ashton may have taken his car, but I was left a couple of very nice, very well-kept cars that went along with the estate. I may not know much about cars, but I know how to drive. Well, kind of.

With that thought, I get dressed and jump in the black Cadillac to take a drive, adjusting the seat so my feet actually touch the pedals. The keys fall out of the visor above my head, and with them a small dried purple flower. One adorned with dried delicate thorns that break upon my touch.

The devil's gift, I seem to recall from some unknown memory looking down at its sad petals. The ring. This flower. All trying to tell me something. Warn me. I put the gearshift in reverse, an overwhelming want to be out of this house being stronger than ever.

It's a nice southern fall night in Louisiana. I roll the windows down as I drive slowly into town. The smell of the air morphs as I continue to coast down the dirt road. The estate smells of earth and damp roots. Town smells like spice, sugar, and secrets. And the feeling you get when rolling through is one of high energy with the eclectic mix of people and food.

There is another feeling here though, and it matches the one I get at the house. The unknown hangs just above my head, permeating my instinct to let me know it's nearby. The veil here feels thin—too thin—like something on the other side is watching back.

My car drives past an old cemetery and halts to a stop without warning. I curse under my breath. I should have checked to make sure the car was working properly before I drove it this far. Or did I even check to see if it had gas?

I turn the key again, but nothing. I look over at the cemetery, its stone tombs teasing me with their promised future. I wonder whether they buried my uncle there. Strange that I've never thought about it until now. I have yet to see his grave. When was his funeral even? Odd that I never heard a thing about it.

That last thought makes me gather my nerve and get out of the car. It is dark now, and I'm thankful I found a flashlight in the glove compartment. The remnants of the dried thistle blow out of the car as I open its door. I watch as they all gather at the base of an established tree. A hickory tree, no less.

I walk the cemetery grounds, waiting to see his name pop up. Nothing. The wind picks up. My gut tells me to walk back toward my broken-down vehicle. A brush of something dense and snake-like moves across my shoe.

I jump up, my heart lodging in my throat. The trees seem different here, as if filled with the souls of the ones laid to rest on these grounds, waiting anxiously for their next fill. The shadows of their branches reach out to grab me.

I hear a twig crunch as if from soft steps. The flashlight flickers as I rush to the car, but I make it. I give the ignition another go, and it spurs to life. *Thank the Gods.* Breaking down next to a cemetery all night is the last thing I need.

I've been driving well over thirty minutes, doing multiple circles around this tiny bayou town. Thinking hard about the fact that my uncle's grave was nowhere to be found. Perhaps they cremated him, but then where are his remains? The thought ruminates in my head until I can hold it no more.

I find a small bar that doesn't even seem as if it's open, but the door swings wide and the sound of conversation over music floats through the open windows of the car. I decide to go in. Maybe a local bar full of strangers is just what I need to clear my mind. It's dark and smoky like the bars of Detroit, but the very jazzy music changes that comparison in an instant.

Full of people all around talking and watching the stage, where a beautiful leggy woman with dark skin is singing a sorrowful tune. Pulling me in as if roots sinking into the bayou. I've never heard a more haunting song. I sit and watch in a trance, like everyone else who is just as captivated by this marvelous melodic creature.

When she is done, she bows and walks offstage. The man, who must own the bar, pops on the mic and tells everyone to give Miss Cypress a round of applause. Even here in the depths of civilization, the trees hold their ownership.

The next act comes on the saxophone, playing a more upbeat, buzzy tune. Its jovial beat making me grasp the reality I find myself in. I look to the bar then, no longer a slave to the song. My drink of choice tonight is a whiskey sour, not my usual, but maybe embracing something new is just what I need.

I feel him before I see him, his eyes fixed from a darkened corner. Ry. Thankfully, the smoky darkness of the bar keeps from revealing the relief on my face that he is here. This man is a drug, and I can't stop with just a taste.

He radiates toxicity, and for whatever reason, I am drawn to it, especially now that he is near. But I don't want him to see the pleasure on my face, not after the way he treated me and then ghosted for weeks, which I guess is just as much my fault as his.

He strolls up behind me, leaning down to whisper in my ear.

"I can't tell whether our meeting like this is a good thing or a bad thing. What do you think?" His breath is hot and smells of caramel bourbon. I love the way his words linger on my skin. I shiver. He must feel me underneath him.

"Mmmm yes, I agree," he purrs, and I can feel him grinning next to my ear.

I spin around on my barstool, thinking he will back up, but he doesn't. Acting as if we haven't just spent weeks avoiding each other. His hands brace the bar over me, so our faces are almost touching as I look up at him. Eyes linked. Mine in defiance, his in challenge.

What our gaze says in those four minutes could fill the room. There is only us, and it has been this way time and time again. But he disrespected my boundaries. Acting as if he held sway in what I do. Who I see. I won't allow it.

His hand reaches to tuck a strand of hair behind my ear, then comes to rest on the dip where my waist meets my hip. *Damn his hands.* I look down at it, wishing him away no longer. *Damn my reaction to him.* He moves his hand down lower to grasp tighter. My body responds. He tips my chin up, so we are eye to eye yet again. *And damn his eyes.*

In a room full of strangers, I can tell it is no coincidence we found each other in this bar tonight. It was always meant to be.

"Let's go," his voice is as rough as his grip, and I can tell he feels as on edge as I do. If I give in now, I'm done for. There is no going back.

Letting my body guide me, I take his hand as he leads me out of the bar and right into his car. And in that moment, I know, I never stood a chance.

24

TOWNHOUSE

RACINE 1978

The moment we are in the car, he puts it in drive. Stillness stretches across the distance between the two front seats. His jaw, held tight as if he is deciding what he wants his next move to be. I know what I want it to be. My want, I hope selfishly, rubs off on him.

His hand grips the steering wheel fiercely, as if he is battling against his own free will. Less than ten minutes later, we park in front of a house that also must double as an office.

Is this his house? The sign on the door confirms it. *Ry Heart Estate Lawyer* it reads in bold white lettering. The quiet eats the air between us for far too long, giving the impression he may not want to see where the next move will take us.

"Well, I guess I'll be getting out then." I say, annoyed at his indecisiveness, which clearly has something to do with the war going on in his head.

The road is empty of traffic, and I get out of the car, looking around. Although it is dark, I can see he lives in a unique part of town screaming of old money. The houses stand tall and strong. Boldly emanating their own level of elegance with their gothic styled architecture.

Ry curses under his breath, and slams the car door as he exits. Here we go again.

"Follow me," he demands. I am not normally one for men bossing me around, but I follow anyway through an odd instinct I've never been compelled to heed before until him.

He is unlocking the door when I decide to put my hand on his arm. The electricity that shoots through us is sharp and unmistakable. A charge not of this world, begging me to touch him again.

"Don't," he growls. This time I *am* put off by his brashness.

"Listen, I don't know who you think you are talking to me that way, but I've had enough. You can't tell me who I can be friends with, where I can go in *my* house or what I can or can't do." He's quiet, so I continue.

"We barely know each other, so I understand you have boundaries. But you are the one who went as far as taking me to your house or whatever this place is. I didn't even want to see you tonight, but there you were." Those last sentences feel like a lie on my tongue, so I decide to say what I know is true next.

"But one thing you cannot deny is this feeling between us. Tell me I'm not wrong?" My anger-filled words lose momentum with the last sentence I spit out when I realize he has backed me against the door frame.

"You're not wrong," he says roughly. And wraps his fingers delicately around my neck. He squeezes slightly, forcing me to lean my head back to look up at his sea-green eyes.

"Then tell me you're sorry," I say strongly, but I can hear my voice break. A daring comment to say to the man who has his massive hand around my throat.

"No." He is still staring me down, swallowing his restraint. For a moment, his eyes question me. Boring their way into my subconscious.

I should be mad at this statement, but something makes me ask,

"Why 'no'? You think you have control over me? Because you don't. You don't own me."

With that, his grip tightens, and his eyes turn dark. My pulse quickens under his large palm. The beat underneath feeling like a catalyst to what I expect will happen next.

"Now that is where you are wrong, my sweet succulent. I *do* own you. Every single inch of you belongs to me. Shall I show you?" He smirks. His eyes turn almost black, and his skin seems to shine gold under the moonlight above us. My eyes widen in response to his words, and the way he seems to physically morph before me.

Still, I say, "Yes. Show me."

His enormous smile is instantaneous. He looks happy, excited, and ravenous, mimicking what he always does best: a hawk swooping toward its prey.

"There's my girl," he whispers. His hand comes off my throat and both move down to grasp my bottom as he lifts me up. I wrap my legs around his waist, and he carries me into the house, slamming the front door behind him. This game of resistance has played out. And the desire we both have is true and fast.

I'm not entirely sure where we head next as our lips keep meeting to say what we know is inevitable. My arms and legs are woven around him, unwilling to let go. He pushes my dress up, and the shock of a cold, hard surface under my thighs makes my whole body arch into him.

I pull my top over my head and, as if he reads my mind, his mouth finds one of my nipples. I hike up my skirt, helping him. Ry finds the edges of my panties and shimmies them down my legs and over my sneakers. Everything happens charged, hungry, and without pause.

"Open up those pretty lips for me," he says, and I'm sure he is talking about my more intimate parts.

I open my legs and move my hand down, but he pins it down to my side. I look up at him, unsure until I see his intent. *Oh.* My panties balled in his fist waiting. I open my mouth, and he stuffs them in.

Surprise hits me when I feel the pooling of moisture between my legs leak onto the countertop. Ry reaches in between my legs with the same hand he used to shove the panties in my mouth. He gently sticks in one finger, slowly playing come-hither with my arousal.

"Do you like the taste of yourself in your mouth? I sure as hell do." He trails kisses down my neck and chest, latching onto my nipple again. His warm tongue curling around my bud. It's so good. Too good. He owns me—there is no doubt.

He pumps another finger into me, stretching me and curling it up. Finding myself not even on the counter anymore as he sucks my nipples, and I shamelessly ride his fingers.

"Keep going," I rasp out through waves.

His thumb circles my clit, while I feel myself breaking around him. But before I burst, he puts me on the floor. Spinning me around and pushing my head down on the smooth marble counter.

My face pressed hard against the surface, and my ass exposed to him. Ry spreads my cheeks apart, and I feel him at my entrance. I open my legs wider—ready. A stinging slap burns on my bottom right before he pounds into me.

I scream in pleasure, but the panties that still fill my open mouth smother it. My bare nipples ache, still wet from Ry's mouth and now raw from the friction. He keeps pounding into me from behind. Slapping the same cheek until I squirm under him. The pain mixes with pleasure, confusing my senses.

"More Ry. I need more." My breathy plea is barely audible, but he hears it. This is a rough rush I am not used to, and it's one I've only now come to know with Ry.

He reaches in between my thighs with his hand and starts pinching my swollen clit lightly. I'm unconsciously meeting his thrusts, helping him get deeper each time. He is giving me what I asked for.

Ry moves his other hand to open my backside up even more, picking up the pace and spitting between my cheeks, letting his saliva run around my tightest spot. He puts his finger there and starts rubbing circles just as he rubs hard on my clit, still stretching me with his huge, wet, thrusting dick.

In seconds, I am gone. I convulse under him and feel an explosion of wetness from where he enters me. He growls at the heat of it, his rhythm turning feral, grabbing a chunk of my ass with his hand and using it to bounce me on and off of his swollen shaft.

He pulls out and releases his load all over my backside. I feel it dripping down into my separation, claiming me. It is then that I realize the truth of what he said earlier. He does have complete ownership over every part of me, and I *want* it that way.

Point made.

FLASHBACK
DACIA 140 & FRANCE 1783

My body rests, but my mind does not.

I'm walking through a large wheat field, adorning an old simple mauve dress, tattered toward the bottom. A sure sign that it's a staple in my wardrobe from whatever era this is.

The setting sun gives a warm glow throughout the sky. A wooden water bucket sits off to the side of a tall, desolate forest. I spin in slow, familiar circles through the golden fields, like I've done this before. I should be home by now, but something about the air keeps me here longer tonight than usual. And the beautiful sunset keeps me longer still.

In my dream, I twirl. My hands brush along the uncut millet stalks. Head directed up toward the sky, eyes closed. I spin slowly, soaking up the warm smell of dirt and dry grass. The sound crunching beneath my feet.

A sharp sensation on my fingers shocks me to a halt. Tiny thorns are embedded in most of my fingertips. Looking around, I see that hidden amongst the wheat are thistle plants. Bright purple flowers look back at me mockingly.

I start pulling each thorn out individually. It is hard with the lack of light, but I remove the last one finally. Tiny dots of blood have surfaced on my fingers, threatening to spill. A couple of drops slide down onto the ground. I wipe the remaining on the earth below, knowing if I get it on my dress my mother will not be pleased.

I feel eyes on me then. It's just a feeling, but it is sure and strong. Goose pimples erupt over my skin. I turn to the woods, knowing whoever is watching me is just within the trees.

I think there is a faint shadow of a man, but the shadow extends into tree branches. My imagination has really gotten the best of me. The ever-watching presence is still there. It feels so vaguely familiar. Personal.

The eyes burn at my skin, as if whoever is looking through them has finally caught their prey. Just then, a hawk swoops out from the woods and knocks me to my behind in bewilderment. I scramble up, collecting my water bucket and sprinting home as fast as my feet will take me.

As I'm running, my dream then morphs into a small party of sorts, and I am not running anymore, but dancing. A sunroom that only shows a gloss of moonlight above, helping to discern that it is clearly nighttime. I know this not only because of the darkness that won't let me see out the windows, but because white moonflowers creep up and line the glass on the outside of the sunroom walls.

There are four of us, including me. Their faces blur at the edges—recognizable, yet not. I can tell there are two men with magnificent builds holding up glasses of wine that keep sloshing out from the movement of their dance. They seem happy, but also delusionally so.

A very young woman lounges on a small chaise. Dark, demonic, but ethereal art surrounds her. I immediately recognize some of the paintings.

One in particular is a painting of a demon sitting on top of an unconscious woman, her arms outstretched over her head in lustful agony. It is from the Romanticism art movement, and I now see all the art has the same dark, romantic feel.

The woman's hand is outstretched toward me now. She is trying to *hand me something. I take it and roll it around my fingers. It is a small seed of sorts. I realize I am under some type of influence. A slow, drugged haze creeps through my veins. Walls cave in around me.*

I look to the girl on the chaise and I can only make out her mouth as she screams.

"LEAVE, Jade, GO!!" A mouth I've seen before. Then I see red coats her throat, and oozes down to her exposed chest. Blood. She is still screaming at me.

"His roots will trap you! GO!!" She is coughing up blood as her words sound muddy, wet and thick. I go to reach for her. To save her, but I'm pulled back by manly arms that wrap around me.

It's then that I wake, heart still racing. Two powerful arms hold me close. My back collides with the shallow breathing of a sleeping man. Ry.

I try to relax into him, but the image of the woman has shaken my mind. I have seen her cherry lips before. I take deep breaths to calm my racing heart, but the drug from my dream still holds its effect.

I can't shake the eerie feeling that the dream was a warning. My finger aches from phantom pricks, along with the emptiness of a ring that calls to me—now more than ever.

25
THE AWAKENING
RACINE 1978

After waking at Ry's townhouse, the dream still fresh in my mind rattles my being and makes falling back to sleep impossible. Ry sleeps like a rock, and it proves easy not to disturb him when I creep out of bed.

I wait for the coffee to brew. Roaming through the rest of the rooms, finding myself lingering in one room in particular. It must be his office, but it is so well kept that I can't imagine someone working here.

No piles of paperwork linger on his desk. There are no law books displayed on the shelves. No trash waiting to be taken out. I'm starting to think this must be his home office, *or* he is neat to the point of obsession.

I'm about to leave when I see a glint of green as my eyes scan his all but bare desk. And it's not just any green. It is a green that belongs to me.

That vibrant green—I know it. Too well. The color being of a certain willow whose pieces lay in a tin inside a drawer of the shop, because I didn't have the heart to throw it away.

I move closer to it on the desk, and I see it is in fact what I've been looking for. More confused than ever, I snatch it up. Anger rises at the thought of why this would be here. Did Ry steal it? What would he want with this ring?

Not wanting to lose it again, I slide it on my ring finger without thinking. In seconds, a thin line of blood forms from my knuckle to its base where I dragged the ring down. But that is not all.

With that one small action, the room starts to twist and bend into darkness. I'm struck with stillness, and then the panic hits me like a ton of bricks.

I'm being swept through every emotion, caught up by giant waves that keep falling into each other before I can catch my breath. Each one taking me deeper into feelings that I hadn't even known in this lifetime—but perhaps in another.

As that thought crosses my mind, I am flooded with memories. Beautiful memories full of laughter with lifelong friends. Friends still known to me in this lifetime. Memories of dancing in a familiar man's arms, dressed in a stunning mauve gown from some time long ago. Even the landscape looks out of this era. From a different time and country altogether.

There are memories of me, two men, and a woman in an art room. We are lounging and taking some sort of drug and then dancing in the moonlight. I flash through castles, fields of wheat, arms I know too well. And then making love.

So much love being made. A caress on my cheek, the sensation of stubble brushing against my skin, teeth nipping at my flesh in the form of ecstasy. That is until the teeth break skin, leaving blood trailing in its path. Feral eyes and a loss of control. A loss of life. My life. Every time.

After that come the memories that aren't so lovely. They are dark, consuming me with their rot and bruising me with their heartache. My own heart feels as if it is being squeezed by a powerful hand and being dripped of every life I watch play out.

I've either died at the hands of myself or a man in every one. Each life ripped away the moment I remembered too much. Every life that has ended in despair being brought on by the same two men. Mostly one in particular, Ry.

My eyes are open now. There are all these memories, but I am still left with broken pieces. The familiar man in this horrid playback is the one that lay in slumber upstairs in bed.

The other is one whose charm oozes out of him into whomever he sets his eyes on. One with moonlit hair and a vulnerability I've never seen in a man before. Que.

The memories are heart-wrenching, and I'm left immobile on the ground, only feeling and replaying these memories in my mind, and then—nothing. I remain. Not wanting to move for fear more memories will surface.

I hear whispers of a voice. It is Ry. He finds me curled in the fetal position on the ground of his office. Tears have stained my cheeks and left my face puffy and numb. My hands, balled into fists, grasp at the shirt fabric near my heart, which is now utterly dismantled.

There will be no going back after this. And what a shame that is, because as I look in the eyes of this man that I've known in so many lifetimes, but am just getting to know in this one—all I see is danger.

When he finds me, at first he holds a look of shock and worry, but then his eyes cast down at my clenching fingers. He must see what's fitted perfectly on my ring finger. I pull myself up onto my palm, fresh tears pooling at my eyes, and one hand still gripping my chest.

"You," I choke out. "Have you known all this time? Is that why you stole my ring?"

A ring that belongs to me and only me. Formed out of lethal love and chaos made from the hands of this very man. A ring I now know my mother must have kept hidden and safe for so many years to keep me away from this man. This very man that has torn my whole being apart for lifetimes on end.

"Explain this!" I all but scream at him. Tears hit the floorboards as I look up to him in angst, hoping what I saw is some mistake. He looks at me unsure, as if he isn't sold on what I now know or don't.

"I took the ring from you for your own safety, Jade," Ry says, and continues, "when you told me it poked you, I knew what it would do, because we've played this game before. So many fucking times." He cradles my hands. For a moment, I let him until I pull them away. I can tell this hurts him. *Good.*

"I couldn't let you find out. Not yet. I wanted more time with you. The real you, not tainted by the past. Not tainted by who we have been to each other." He sighs. He has been here before. Same woman, different time. "But the past always creeps in life after life...I hoped this one could be different."

"I saw...I saw it all," I mumble out. I cast my eyes down now at the ring. The ring that fits the box and a door in the basement of a house I now own. I see the memories of my many lives on earth and who was in them—how they ended.

But what I don't see is what's behind the doors, who is this man that I've spent all these lives with? And Que, he was in just about every life, too. How can this be? To live so many lives with the same people by my side in each?

"I need to go," I say as I try to stand up, wobbling on my legs that almost can't support my weight. Perhaps it is the weight of knowing that is causing me to drag? All I want to do is go process everything, and sleep. I want to sleep so badly. I want to sleep with all that I am.

"No," Ry says low and dangerous. "That is not a good idea. I think you should stay. We should talk this out." Ry looks at me.

I see the pain and anguish in his eyes begging me to stay, but there is something deeper, too. Something scarier within, as his panic turns to fear. I try to walk away, but Ry grabs tight onto my wrist. So tight I feel my ligaments stretch in an unnatural disconnecting.

"Please," he whispers.

But I can't. I need comfort without confusion, and that is something Ry cannot give me right now. So, I pull away from him and head toward the door. He slams it closed just as I open it, pushing me against it; pinning me.

There was a time before when one of us was in the dark about who we are to each other, but now I see him. I see what I turn him into. I see how he breaks me into pieces over and over in every life.

He holds my gaze, and my whole body pleads to run. He pushes himself against me. His kind demeanor turning into something unhinged. The switch has flipped, and Mr. Hyde makes his appearance.

"You see, my sweet succulent. I'm not sure you saw everything when you put that ring on, but one thing you should know is that you *are* mine. You were made for me. Every. Single. Part. Of *you*." He holds me by my ribs under my shirt. I feel his thumb grazing my flesh.

And as scared as I am by the look in his eye, I am his. I can feel this to my core, and it makes me sick. Sick of who I would become for this man. Sick of who I became in all my other lives for him until he eventually became my undoing.

If I learned anything from those memories that filled my head just moments ago, it's that sometimes, love won't set you free. Sometimes, it will bind you to a life of confusion and self-loathing. A cage of toxicity making you question every aspect of your being. And this is a love like that.

Without warning, Ry's lips are on mine. I feel a sharp pinch, along with the taste of metal in my mouth. His eyes go wild, hungry, savage. I am terrified, and he can tell. He is feeding off my terror.

For her blood is the blood of the trees, and every Being wants a taste.

The sentence burns into my consciousness. Whose words haunt me now? Mine? My mother's? All I know is that this is too much.

"Ry stop," I gasp, "I'm afraid...you're scaring me."

Ry lets out a low chuckle, and his eyes spark, turning from sea foam green to an ominous bark black color. The color of roots smothered in the earth's soil, growing stronger in darkness.

"I know you're afraid, Jade. I can feel it. Fear is nothing new to me. Everyone fears me." He caresses my skin with his dark words.

"What *are* you?" I say in a fast, shallow breath. Still pinned to the door.

I don't think I saw everything there was to see in those visions. Things are missing. Important things. Ry smiles then. It's evil, and I see his markings solidify.

The scars on his head move as if they are hiding something beneath. More of the same deep markings now grow around those scars, which form what can only be described as a shadow of tendrils, much like the roots of a hickory tree—then he speaks.

"There are some who would consider us demons, some of us who act more like fae, and some who would argue we behave like the gods. But we are more than that." He bites the words into my ear.

This I know. I've felt in my essence all along. My connection to the trees. My connection to him. But I ask anyway.

"And what is *that*?" I'm afraid of his next words. I shouldn't be, knowing that they are a part of me. His eyes twinkle with dark magic.

"We are the Beings beneath the roots," he answers, as if this knowledge is known to all.

I act as if I know, not wanting to let him feel as if he has the upper hand.

"You aren't the only one from whom I've felt fear, my sweet succulent. I've felt it my whole life." He breathes me in, using my terror as a life force. I wriggle against him, trying to gain some leverage to decide my next move. Flee or stay.

"A life that has lasted longer than I care to admit. A life so long that I've stopped caring about anything that isn't this anger swarming inside of me." He looks at me, and I would think he was concerned with this declaration about his life. His aggressive facade falters before he says more.

"Don't you see, I am feared because I don't give a shit." He slams his palm against the door right next to my head. "Make me give a shit,

Jade. I dare you." His words are angry and speak of violence, but I can feel in his tone, a misplaced bitterness. Sorrow for what he has had to become.

I am about to go where I know I shouldn't. Into the depths of his gaze, wanting to wrap my fingers in his hair, but wanting to run away at the same time. Looking into his magnetic, otherworldly eyes, everything seems like a dream. Or a nightmare—which one it is at this point, I can't tell.

Have I really lived one real moment since I put the ring on? But the metallic blood on my lip is a brutal reminder that this is true. My feelings are true. However, I trust nothing and no one right now.

I am saved by a knock at the door. And Ry looks at the clock on the wall. His eyes flash with frustration as he tries to calm himself. He steps back from me, returning to a cool, thinly masked demeanor as he opens the door.

To my surprise, an older gentleman stands at the door and gives us both a nod.

"Good morning," he says brightly. He looks me over. I know I must look like hell, so I smile back and politely excuse myself. Fast and calmly, I grab my purse and shoes.

Ry and the older man seem to start in a deep discussion, so I use this as my excuse to sneak past them. Ry eyes me, not wanting me to leave, but I know I need to get away while I still have the chance. The older man looks at me again kindly and continues talking, showing no signs of letting Ry out of their conversation.

Taking a strained walk back to the main road of the town, I can finally catch my breath. I look down at my finger adorning the ring, and it shimmers, feeling at home once and for all. Too bad it's a broken home.

I can't help but think about the other ring spot in that box I found. Where and to whom does that belong? Why didn't I see anything regarding that?

I move faster, putting as much distance between me and Ry as I can. I feel so full of memories of past lives. One knocking into the next. I need the answers to sort out this mess in my head, and I know just who to ask.

There were two other people in those memories of lives lived I trust with all my heart. I need to find my way back to them to unearth the truth. Even if it means questioning all that they are to me.

26

TELL ME EVERYTHING
DETROIT 1978

I enter my shop in the early morning hours the next day. Even the city, apart from the auto factories humming, sleeps when I arrive. I left with little thought, only grabbing Carya and locking the front door of what I now saw as a fractured estate.

I should not have driven in the state that I was, so desperately in need of sleep and a hug. One clove after another, just to stay awake. I look at my hand. The cold, comforting feeling of a ring that looks dull and weighed down by all the hope it's lost.

The only thing going through my mind now is the answers I desperately seek. Two people hold those answers, and I only hope that their keeping me in the dark had good reason.

Looking at the items in the shop now brings a new feeling of nostalgia. These aren't just items on display to sell. No, these are not just antiques. They're echoes. Each one a mess I lived through.

Past beloved treasures. How could I not have seen it before? Is that why I searched them out? By a feeling? An invisible tether of truth I was chasing?

A cracked floral vase from Ry that once held a promise in the form of sharp, thorny flowers. The first edition Frankenstein book that marked the moment I discovered his watchful eyes for the first time in Racine. A Scottish coin—just enough to buy a room, and a little time to fall apart.

And the paintings. The paintings Ry and Que would bring back to me from their travels abroad as soldiers—at least that is what I believed then. All just things, but more than that to me now.

A key part of the best moments with Ry is here, so many failed attempts at keeping our tainted love from becoming sour. These possessions hold my connection to that past. A past I can't escape. Maybe part of me never wanted to.

I am left thinking, even crying when the feeling of weakness holds me hostage. I finally notice the sun has risen over the city as light starts to filter into the shop windows. I put on a pot of coffee, wiping the leftover drops of heartache out of my vision.

The caw of the crows is a welcome noise, but even it holds a different meaning now. There is something about the birds. Their watchful eyes, a vessel for someone else. And I now know who.

The hawk, a silent and deadly overseer for Ry. And the crow, a noisy observer for Que. This much I know, but how its possible is still foggy.

Carya is curled up in her bed in the corner of the store, like she never left. Maybe we should never have left. Lollie should be here any moment to open up the shop, and I know I'm the last face she will expect to see.

At 7:55 a.m., I hear the door jingle and the chime ring as Lollie lets herself in. She looks up, feeling my anguish immediately. I must shock her. The last time I looked in the car mirror, dark circles wore like war paint under my sunken eyes.

With a mix of exhaustion and mascara bleeding down, making me look like something that just crawled out of a grave. In a haunting way, I guess that's exactly what I've been doing life after life. Crawling out of my own dreary grave over and over, brain full of mush, hoping I can live a normal life.

"Oh, Jade," she runs to me, and cups my head in her hands. Tears fall before I can even try to hold them back. "Oh, my dear Jade." She speaks as if she knows. I look to her then, and her eyes tell me she does.

"Please. Enough with the secrets. I need to know everything," I say.

She gets up and locks the door, coming back to sit with me on the floor. She takes my hands in hers, threading her fingers through mine, and for a moment we sit in silence.

I look to her, love and wonder mixing with anger, defiance and mistrust. My shoulders straighten, and my eyes lock onto hers.

"I'm ready. Tell me everything."

27

INFORMATION OVERLOAD

DETROIT 1978

"Y ou've had numerous human lives with us before he found you on Earth. I'll start with the first one he made his presence known. That may be the easiest way to go about this. It was Dacia in 140 AD, which is now known as Romania," Lollie says solemnly. Her first words pull the air from my lungs.

"Things were simple then. You lived in a quiet village, surrounded by love—your mother and me. But you started staying out longer. Every evening you would go get water from the well until one day you just didn't come back. We searched forever, it seemed." Her confession tugs at my knowing.

"I've seen this in my dreams. The wheat field with hidden thistle," I say more to myself.

"All we found was the water pail close to the edge of the woods. And instead of water in the pail, there was only blood. You were gone to us." Lollie's eyes gloss over remembering. I can tell it's hard, but she continues. "And we were broken, thinking you were gone forever. We didn't know you would come back as a mortal again, whether he found you or not."

"But instead, I've been set up to live out this torment, life after life…" I look at her, tears swelling with rage. How could she not know the pain this would cause?

"That's not fair. We were trying to give you freedom. Your mother wanted you to live." I scoff at her words. Lollie doesn't realize their contradiction. They wanted me to live, but I feel like I die a million times every time I slip that ring on.

"We tried, Jade. To keep you safe. We knew we had to try harder. But in the next life in Scotland, he gave you that ring. Now, no matter how hard we tried to keep an eye on you, you found your way to each other. But at least this time we had something to bury." And as she mentions it, I feel overwhelmingly conscious of the circle around my finger. Of the power he forged into it.

I turn my head, and close my eyes tight. Tears stinging at the corners. Not wanting to think about the last part she mentioned.

"So, you were there?" I ask, even though I know what her answer will be.

"Yes, Jade, I was. I was always there along with your mother. We tried harder each time to keep him from finding you. Sometimes it worked, but others…well, you were eventually lost to us," Lollie says.

"There are details I've lost…" I stammer. There is so much I don't understand. I remember the events of my past lives, but what exactly the others are seems just out of grasp.

"Let me explain more. In another life, we found you in France… the Romantic era. I could tell you were fond of this time. You lived fully and unapologetically." Lollie smiles at this.

I remember dancing with friends under the careful watch of the glowing moon. Some warm memories come to me, but I realize they were forever fleeting.

"We became very good at finding you at the start of each of your lives. Your birth mother never survived—for your soul was never fully anchored to her. Your true mother always found you, with me by her side. It's one gift of being us. And being you."

"So why did she leave me? If she is so gifted as you say..." I feel betrayed and, even worse, I feel deserted.

"Willows can't survive long away from water, love." She looks at me then, knowing exactly what comes to mind. Our late-night drives to the countryside. The memory warms me, but what does it have to do with my mother leaving?

Lollie continues, reminding me of all the memories that surfaced on Ry's townhouse floor.

"In that life you lived a life of privilege, so we could always have our eye on you. But through the war, he found you. This time as a soldier. We did our best to watch your every waking moment, but in the end—we failed again. Even worse than before. They both found you then." Lollie's face grows dim.

She speaks of Ry and Que, in a time when they were friends.

"They turned you into something you were not, Jade. I thought Carya cared for you more than what he let happen. Quercus found Jimsonweed on one of his travels abroad." Lollie's eyes water at the memory, as she absentmindedly spins a creamy iridescent stone ring around on her right finger.

I quickly remembered my vision of the room full of art. The two men with me and another woman. The white moonflowers creeping up the windows, and the feeling of hallucinating. This must be the life she speaks of.

My head throbs. To know these visions I've had all my life were not straying me from reality, but actually were my reality.

"So, Quercus must be Que, but why do you call Ry that? Carya. That is my cat's name." I ask, still trying to grasp onto bits and pieces and linking them to my memories, visions and what Lollie is laying out in front of me.

"Why do you think you named your cat that, Jade? The subconscious can do a number on our tangible lives. Carya is Ry's full name." She pauses, causing my mind to go back, trying to remember.

Why *did* I name my cat Carya? It was just an odd name that just popped into my head, but perhaps it was more than that. A link.

She continues, "It is also another name for *Hickory*."

Hickory? The book I read at the estate comes to mind. Why didn't I see it before? I can tell Lollie is deciding whether she should continue, but she does.

"This is where things will get a little weird, so bear with me. Try to remember. Carya is not of this world, but of a world beneath the roots." Yes, I know. She goes on, "The Rooted Realm. He rules the realm below..."

"The hickory tree," I interrupt her in a whisper. I had felt it all along.

"Yes, good. He is an ancient being with more power than any human could fathom—and you were his way to have more." My heart wrenches at her statement.

At this point, not much can shock me, but this does. I've seen so much play out in the fabric of my being since putting the ring on. I know what she says is true, but why couldn't I access his name before? I must say this aloud, because Lollie responds.

"Since you are in a mortal body, not all memories are available to you about your past lives. The Beings have authority that way, and the curse put on you has restrictions we could not change because of your being rooted in the realms beneath."

"But what about you? Who are you? My mother. She is connected to the willow. I know this." I think of the small magnolia tree Lollie planted next to her house. The one in front of the estate. It clicks.

"My true name is Magnolia, but I've grown used to Lollie by now. Your mother Sal, short for Salix, another name for Willow, which is what your soul recognizes her as. We are both lesser tree Beings," Lollie says and smiles softly.

My universe stops. A flood to my system. I knew this in my bones all along. My mother and the tree I hold dear with all my heart are one and the same.

"But then why did my mother die, yet you are still here?" She must read the confusion on my face.

"We need to be near our trees to survive on this land, and there aren't many willows in Detroit. The one by the cemetery was our closest, but even that was too far. And that last time we paid it a visit, her life force was just too low already." I think of how my mother faded every year.

I know this is hard for her to talk about, just as it is hard to hear.

"You have heard her, I believe. She always tries to come through to you." Lollie lets the last part sink in before she continues. "That is also why we have Ash. He came after your third life of being found went into such disarray. We knew we needed help." That much is clear, I think.

Lollie keeps going, "Ash is a tree Being your mother and I trusted. We still do. It shouldn't be hard for you to guess which rooted realm he rules over." Lollie winks at me, but her humor is lost in my mistrust, and rightly so. I still have so many questions, but I ask the one weighing most on my mind.

"But what does Carya, no Ry, want with me?" His name feels funny on my tongue, when the only Carya I've known is my orange stray tabby, perched in the corner feeling my desperation from across the room.

"The same thing that all the higher tree Beings want. Your blood." She looks down then.

"Your blood would make any tree Being reek of power, but you were promised to Carya. Your mother and I just wanted to protect you. We couldn't stand by and watch your essence be drained." She eyes me intently. Hoping I understand. "We cast your spirit into a stone to keep you safe." At the mention of a stone, the one on my ring shimmers. I can't seem to take it off.

"It wasn't a simple choice. There were setbacks that Willow

couldn't live with. With some help, we tied your soul to a mortal life. By breaking the stone, you were free to be reborn in human form," Lollie's words weighted.

Realization sets in. This was the stone. Pieced back together by Ry. For the sake of love or ego? Could it be both? Placing it on made me remember. Part of me wished it didn't.

"It wasn't perfect, but it kept you safe—until now," Lollie looks at the ring on my left hand. "Inlaid with thistle thorns, so he can find you once your blood marks the earth. Even a drop. Or, as you've found out, once you put it on—you remember." Just like that. My entire world falls apart with putting the wrong ring on the right girl.

"Either way, it's disastrous. For your mind. For his hunger for you." She focuses on me then with caring eyes that have seen me at my best, and apparently my worst.

"I...just..." My brain hurts. How could the life that I thought I knew everything about turn around with just the slip of a ring? My mind is a mess, cracked open, leaking all the bits I can't hold any longer. Lollie must see this.

"Let's head home, Jade. I think you need to rest. I'll have Ash come by with some food." She pulls her coat over my shoulders. It's colder here. "We can talk more, but I think right now you just need a break from everything. You need sleep."

With her arm around my shoulder, I feel like a child again. I lean into her. Focusing on one small but crucial detail—in the end, *no one is who they seem.*

28

DREAMLAND ETHER

DETROIT 1978

I sit at the base of an old willow by a lake long lost to time. In a distant life. Or maybe this life. It's hard to know when you've had so many, for they each bleed into the next.

It is no wonder human lives are so short in retrospect, for they would never hold the memories of what really mattered together if they lived beyond one hundred. They would jumble them all, much like keeping track of a grain of sand on a beach full of a million others.

However, there is a memory that never fades. Not for me at least. It is the memory of my mother. The way she smells like softness and comfort, like her newly made bed that as a child I would dive into until I got lost amongst the mounds of pillows and blankets.

The creases of her eyes when she smiles, permanently etched there from all the times she held a smile so long just looking at me as if I were her whole world. Her hands. Long, slender fingers like the boughs of a willow tree. And her hugs. Hugs that would hold me forever until I decided to let go.

And she is here now. I can feel her as I skim my feet against the water. With one hand planted behind me on the earth and the other on the smooth root of the willow, I feel the vibration pulsating through. It's been alive all this time. She has been alive all along.

She enters my mind effortlessly, and it makes me wonder if the ring was the answer to bring her closer all along.

'It was never the ring, my beautiful girl—it was always you. I've never been apart from you; you've only just awakened.'

Her voice drifts into me like a mourning dove's song, and I wait calmly to hear it again.

'I know this must be hard to accept. Every life, I'd hope would get easier to keep him away, but the memories only got messier. I am so sorry. Sorry too that there is no way to break this spell. If I had known that then, maybe I would have done it differently. But fear took over. Fear of losing you.'

In this dreamland ether, I cannot speak, although I want to. My questions don't come out, and I have so many. Why did you leave? I try to say, but the words don't form. I can listen only. So, I do.

'When you were created, you were born from me. It is only out of true love and hope that one can be created. But right away the realms knew, because being a tree sprite meant you were bound to provide power to another. It was the way of the realm, having been that way for as long as I can remember.'

I try to reach for her voice, but my fingers are only greeted by the mist her words leave behind.

'You were bound to the Rooted Realm of Hickory and Heart before you were even fully formed. Dark earth magic has its ways of getting what it wants, and his heart was the darkest. And it yearned for *you*.'

Ry's hungry look is all I can see. Her words are truer than she knows.

'But I knew your worth wasn't meant to feed some godlike hunger. You see, the realm I oversee is the Rooted Realm of Willow and Worth. And I was going to make sure you saw yours.'

There is nothing from her for so long, I almost think she won't continue. I can feel sadness fill the void. It is hers.

'At least while time was on my side, I wanted you to live without being someone else's means to power. Hiding you so that one day you could find your own power. Find out how worthy you really are.'

Of course, Willow and Worth. My finger trailed its origin from that fragile but enchanting book. The comfort of finding her name amongst the endpapers wasn't just a silly vice—it was true. She was rooting for me all along.

'I wanted you to discover your soul on your own. Because I know your soul, honey. I am of your soul. But unfortunately, so is he.'

29
EXPLANATION
DETROIT 1978

I wake and instantly feel the loss of my mother all over, but instead of a panic-stricken loss, a serene state enters my being. My mother's words always had that effect on me, and the dream of her was no different.

I hear the soft chattering of two voices in the next room as the familiar dark grey couch of my beloved Detroit living room cradles me within it. Parts of me remember driving here with Lollie, but I was in a whirlwind of emotion that I barely know how I came to be back in Detroit in the first place.

I sit up on the couch, squinting to adjust my eyes to the light shining in from the adjoining room, which houses the dining table and chairs. Lollie and Ashton sit at two of them, mumbling in hushed voices. When they notice my movement, they both turn. Lollie smiles, gathering herself up to walk to me.

"Jade. How are you? All rested up, I hope." Lollie says, her outward love and peppiness warming me. She is still upbeat, but there's a new softness in her voice—one I've never heard before. It is almost maternal, which sounds weird coming out of her youthful image. Maybe it's been there all along. I manage a smile.

"Ash brought over some soup from that deli you love. And some beer. Guinness. He thought you might need that more." Lollie rolls her eyes in Ashton's direction. At least some things haven't changed.

I look towards Ashton, and he nods, knowing I need quiet. Always knowing what I need. Even when his roles in each life looked different, he was always my protector.

I get up and make my way to the food. My body aches, but my mind was rewarded with the rest it needed. With food in my stomach, I hope I'll start to feel like myself again. Though I know I can never go back to who I was.

Ashton eyes me, waiting for me to say something, but it feels good to be in silence. So, I eat with both of them giving me the grace to talk when I am ready. It's finally after I've had a sip of the dark beer that I break the ice.

"My mother came to me," I say matter-of-factly. "In a dream last night. She explained some things." After taking another spoonful of soup, I look them over before saying, "But I still have questions."

"And we are here to answer them. The ones we can, at least." Lollie says, her reassuring voice confirming it was the right decision to come back to the two people who know me best.

"OK," I begin, "what's with the house? In Louisiana? My uncle?" I look to them. In all this time they were explaining about keeping me away from Ry, or whatever his name is, they let me go straight to the town he resides in, so there must be something with the house I inherited.

"I can answer that." Ashton straightens his back and rests his forearms on the table. "The house was built by the lesser Beings of Rooted Realm. A safe haven for us to converge together from time to time. We all lived there at one point, protecting you as a child."

Ashton lets the information sit. I'm putting the pieces together. He talks about my previous life right before the one I find myself in now.

"Until after your eighteenth birthday when Carya found you, I believe you know him as Ry. He staked claim over the house.

Sneakily stole it outright from under us." Ashton pulls his fingers into a fist. Always calm, even when anger bubbles up.

"Que soon moved in with him. You see, they were friends once upon a time, but that was the house that broke them. You broke them." Ashton's words sound harsh, although I know he doesn't mean it. It is just the truth.

I think of Ry's silent battle over these past months. Was he trying to be decent? To push me away—to save us? Or was it just a game? I wonder if even he knew the answer to that. Ashton continues, as if seeing the wheels in my mind turning at full speed.

"Ry loved you fiercely, but he knew his hunger for your blood's power would win in the end. And Que, he grew bored. Until I think he started to feel something for you himself. But it wasn't true love..."

"Because I only belonged to Ry. He said it himself." The words tumbling out of my mouth. I wish I would've kept them in, sadly still unsure if I can trust my two dearest friends.

"Yes, your being promised to Ry gave him power over your soul, but you also had power over his, which I didn't think he expected." No, he didn't, I think to myself as Ashton keeps talking.

"Que saw this, and he knew he could use it to make Ry jealous. He told you something he shouldn't have. Trying to break Ry and gain your trust. He ended up doing the opposite." The girl on the bridge. Cutting her arm. The visions were all real, and now I can place them, since I now know I lived them.

"A few weeks later, you ended your life. You said only your mother, and the earth held a claim over your blood. And you drained yourself of it by the bridge in town," Ashton's voice is shaky.

"I saw this. I saw my death, many times. Too many," I say to them.

"You washed up at the willow tree on your property. When Ry found you, he dragged you to his hickory, but you had no blood left. There was no power for him to take," Ashton explains.

I saw this too. It is all coming back clearer now that sleep doesn't plague my mind. How could I live so blindly, and how could my friends let me? I try to absorb what Ashton says next.

"But the power *you* had over him cracked his ego and his heart. He was so broken he cursed himself to never feel anything for you again, which obviously didn't work completely, given the situation we find ourselves in today."

Oh, but this is new. So, he does have a heart.

"Your mother wept more than I ever saw. It tore all of us up. It did every time." Lollie explains, twirling the ring on her finger. Old habits die hard.

"OK, but why would you let me go back there? To the house where this all happened?" I ask.

"Free will, Jade," Aston explains. "You are mortal. It is the one thing we can't control. We can try to dissuade or persuade you, but in the end, it's your choice." It can't be that easy, can it? "If we told you before you were ready, it would've caused more harm than good—that is, if you even believed us. Ry knows this. He saw an opportunity when the groundskeeper passed to get you back to that house."

Ashton breaks, then adds, "the groundskeeper who is of no relation to you at all. Just some sorry soul they trapped to do their bidding, while they hunted you down."

30
BROKEN ESTATE
RACINE 1979

After that, my time only consisted of being at my shop. Lollie and Ash would come by and see if I needed anything, but mostly, gave me my much-needed space. My only true company was from Carya, my forever feline companion whose name will never change. She was the only one not deceiving me, after all.

Even the birds put me on edge—they always had, but now I know why. And so, Carya really is the only one I can depend on in the end. Imagine that. Named by my subconscious, forever linking me to my promised and everything he represents without either of us having a clue.

It had been months since the truth seeped into me like that of encroaching rot seeping into a carcass the crows circle on the street—unwelcome and slowly taking over my whole being. My visions and dreams have faded, thankfully. But I entered a catatonic state of life, and didn't want to know any more of the truth. That was until Cher called my shop.

Her breathless voice over the phone told me the estate was in shambles. Apparently, it had stormed repeatedly since I left. Cher, coming to check on me, saw I was gone and decided to keep an eye on it.

How she got the number of the shop, I do not know. I had no plans of going back to that place. But my bones ached with the sensation that I was yet again not making decisions of my own. Once again, fear and stagnation were calling the shots. I didn't want that, and my soul started to spark to life again.

"You must come back, Jade. Don't let your beautiful estate suffer. It's absolutely broken without you. Plus, I miss you." It was with those words that something in me snapped. I felt betrayed by two men, but I was betraying myself by hiding my worth and not living where I truly felt was my home.

My mother's words came to me then about finding my worth and owning my power. Cher's call rekindled something within that made me feel like I had a whole life ahead of me, as well as decisions to make.

I found myself again in a déjà vu like moment of packing up Carya, a few clothing items, some cherry brandy, and the fated jade ring that I couldn't take off. I left a note on the table for Lollie and Ashton telling them I'm sorry I had to leave without a goodbye, but I needed to fix this.

The car my uncle left me, who apparently wasn't even my uncle for that matter, sat patiently waiting for me to make my next move. So, I left—back to the estate that had changed everything.

Hours of driving and quite a few clove breaks later, a guilty pleasure that is now turning more into a habit, get me to my destination. I slept in the car at a rest stop, Carya curled up in my lap, before I made it the rest of the way, but I made it back.

Finally, I pull up to the house, anticipation digging its claws into my gut. The estate looks unremarkable. Nothing has changed that I can see from where I stare up through the front windshield.

Cher is waiting for me on the porch. She had insisted on camping out when I told her I would be on my way, and from the looks of it—she did exactly that. Her dramatic embrace greets me like a long-lost friend, which isn't that uncharacteristic of her personality. But somehow, this feels truer than most.

"I need to show you something," she exclaims. "And before you say anything, yes, the house is actually fine, but it has been storming, so I wasn't completely lying." So I was right in my assumption that the house looked just the same as I had left it.

"So what, you lied because you missed me?" I say, taken aback that she would lie to me and that she is so good at it, just like everyone else. But her telling me the house was falling apart was not the real reason I drove back, and I know that. The reason is deeper. The reason—a man I numbed myself not to think about these last few months.

"Well, actually my full name is Cherry, and that's another part of my intentions in getting you back here. But I have something to show you first." She says like it's no big deal, leading me up to the front door of the estate.

That is when it dawns on me. Cherry. Like the tree. I *have* seen her before. Rarely, but I saw her there. I'm about to say something when she interrupts.

"Wait, please," she pleads. "Just open the door and let me show you what I think you need to see." And I do. Something in her eyes seems so desperate, but not in a scary way that I've come accustomed to with the other tree Beings that lurk around this town.

As we walk into the house, I let Carya free to wander and follow Cher, or Cherry, I guess it is. For the sake of my sanity, she will stay Cher to me. She leads me up the stairs and up to the attic, as if she knows this house like the back of her hand.

Once in the attic, she pulls a small door open I must have overlooked when I was too preoccupied clearing stuff out with Ry. He invades my thoughts again, awakening them to the feelings that remain unresolved.

"Watch your head," she says as she bends down and disappears through the tiny door. I follow suit behind her, jaw dropping to the floor as I step into a room that holds the most magnificent art. Original art from the Romantic era that must be worth more than a small fortune.

I gasp silently at its beauty. I'd seen this art before on display in the room with all the windows. The reflection of us dancing off its oiled surface. I remembered the men instantly, because they were in almost every memory, but it took a moment to remember the other woman, until now. It was Cher. Cher was with me and Que—and Ry.

And, as if knowing my thoughts, she bows, "I didn't think I'd be that hard to forget," she winks, "and like I said, most call me Cherry, as in The Rooted Realm of Cherry and Choice. And that is what I am here to help you do. Remind you that you *still* have a choice."

"A choice about what?" I ask.

"A choice about your life, of course. And how you want to live it. It is yours after all, and your mother fought quite hard to make sure you have one...or more than one obviously." She says with a flick of her hand, as if this is all perfectly normal.

"But aren't you out to get me like all the other tree Beings? You are with Que constantly...he..." I say, hinting toward her obvious bias.

"Ah yes, he has played a part in a few of your demises. But can you blame him? It's been you and Ry all along. Ry has *never* helped him find his promised, only parades his and yours around like a taunting bully. It was only right he played a game or two." She says this all rather calmly.

I look at her in disbelief. His *games* ended in my death. And more than once. She doesn't seem to notice my distress. She can't be that insensitive, but what do I know of any of these Beings?

"He is the one suffering most, I mean, apart from you right now." She looks at my confused face. "Wait, do you not know? You aren't the only one, sweet girl. Que has a promised as well, and he swore an oath with Ry they would find her. An oath Ry hasn't kept." Another like me? The other ring.

"Que was close to finding her once, with help from you actually. Maybe that is why he has grown so smitten with you after all these centuries together." The more I learn, the more I feel spited by the ones around me.

Cher continues on, not a care regarding the look of unease on my face.

"What happened to her?" I have a sudden uncontrollable need to save her from what I've been put through.

"It didn't work out for him, obviously. They hid her away. I'm surprised she didn't tell you, although in your heart I'm sure you know." Cher tilts her head, intrigued with revealing this bit of information.

"She?" I ask.

"Yes, Magnolia," she answers. "Or what is it you call her... Lollipop or something that?"

"Lollie?" I ask. I can see amusement in her eyes and how pleased she is with herself. She smiles slowly.

"Yes, Lollie," she says, rolling the double l with her tongue. "She can be a mysterious one. But that makes her one hell of a mother. Although is she giving her daughter a choice? I'd probably have to disagree on that one."

"Wait, Lollie has a daughter too...that was promised to Que?" I ask, confirming what I think I just heard. "She didn't tell me."

"Well, love, you don't have the best track record for making decisions regarding yourself *or* her daughter for that matter." Cher comes off cold then. She isn't wrong, but I fight it anyway.

"No, that's not true." I say angrily, tears brimming my eyes.

"It is dear. But you are far from her now. You have a choice. So, what will you choose?" She asks, then pauses, ducking out of the short attic hideaway. Have I ever really had a choice?

"Call if you want to get a drink. I've been needing some more excitement around here, and *you* are sure to deliver," she says in her singsong voice and breezes out the door of The Rooted Realm Estate. The name of this giant place taking on a whole new meaning.

31
DANCING WITH TWO DEVILS
RACINE 1979

I get right drunk that night. And all by myself, for that matter. I don't trust anyone except the cozy feline curled around my feet at the end of the chaise lounge.

It doesn't matter whether I am here or in the upper half of the country. Nobody has been completely truthful with me. Even as my phone rings nonstop, most likely Lollie or Ashton, I replay all the facts over and over in my head, trying to make sense of things I may never fully understand.

Who is this other promised, and why do I feel a tug in my heart when I think about her? It's an ache that has been there all along perhaps, and I am just noticing it now. Crawling out of my subconscious like something unwelcome, but persistent. Is she somewhere out there in human form like me?

I know that both Ry and Que have played their fair share of destructive parts in all of my lives, but perhaps I had just as much to do with those events. My heart being only confused because of how Ry conflicts with the version I knew before I put the ring on. I must move past that. See him for what he is. So many parts good, but *so much bad.*

He lied to me. Broke my mind *and* my body. Even now, his intensity portrays care—written on both our souls, whether or not we admit it. Our story, written over and over in the human world, but rooted in the realms beneath the earth. Does that make it less genuine or, in fact, more? I know I can choose what it means to me.

Then there is Que. His vulnerability in the basement. All the time we spent together in past lives that have only now resurfaced in my memories. He's both friend and villain, depending on where you stand.

He is hurting just as we all are. And maybe even more so. If he found his promised, would he act the way Ry does with me? And all these important people in my life that I am just learning again who they really are to me. Who are they all truly?

It is with that thought that my eyes get heavy from the third cherry brandy I poured myself before I crawled into the long chair with Carya. The chaise that reminds me of the one Cher laid on under the moonlight in France, because it probably is.

My eyes close completely, and I am greeted by the box that holds two rings—meant to hold two stones. One is the one I currently wear on my finger—customized with hickory leaves and thistle thorns that I now know were made to pierce my skin. A rather morbid addition made so Ry can always find me.

The other is of a beautiful moonlit stone. I am no expert in rare gems, but if the moon were to be splashed with the waves from the ocean on a clear star-filled night, then this ring would capture it perfectly.

I watch as the jade ring is placed on my finger, pinching from the small thorns puncturing my skin. *Is true love meant to hurt like this?* I hear a small voice saying in my mind. My voice.

And another. *But what is love without pain? Is it truly interesting if it doesn't hurt a little?* A male voice now, brimming with darkness.

It is Ry, but as I look up my eyes meet the moonlit acorn ones of

Que. He spins me around in my dream. I am floating, and when I spin to meet him again, Ry is back in his place. And that is how the dream continues, on and on. One man becoming the other. I don't know what it means—only that I keep dancing. Dancing with two devils.

32
WORDS HURT
RACINE 1979

When I wake, my stomach is in knots. It wrenches together from all the downloads I've been receiving through my dreams and through the recollections of others. But to be honest, the sourness that meets my stomach and the heaviness that consumes my legs are definitely from the alcohol I had last night after having a self-proclaimed pity party with my dear beloved cat.

I vaguely remember the dream from last night. Could I have feelings for both Ry and Que? I'm not even sure what I should call them. Ry, Carya, Hickory? Que or Oak? What are their true names?

With Que, I hold this understanding of losing something you can't find, much like my memories every time I reincarnate. Whereas my feelings for Ry are a bullet fast and piercing, ripping apart at my soul so that it is all I know. I know they are both men whose morals are almost nonexistent, but that doesn't mean they're unworthy of love.

On that note, I do in fact make a decision of my own. I decide to visit Ry, because for him my feelings are sure. A fated love that must find a way not to end in disaster as it has done in all our other lives together.

My heeled boots click up the steps to Ry's townhouse. I am so scared from my last meeting with him, but that was because of all I did not know and all I felt toward him. He masked his sorrow over our fate with something darker—rage, cruelty. A disillusion I won't let persuade me again.

I knock on the blue-green painted door, trying to make my knuckles sound sure and optimistic. The knob clicks, bringing the door open to reveal who stands behind it. The Ry who greets me is a very different Ry from the one I left months ago. A rigid, tired shell of a man stands before me now.

"I heard you were in town. Wanting to sell after all?" His coldness takes me back to our last meeting. The words of Gerry Rafferty float out the door to me. A mood that doesn't match. But I note that it really has always been me, as the song suggests.

"Can I come in?" I ask hesitantly. Our confrontation feels like an atom bomb at the moment, and my words are the very unstable charge that could set him off.

"Now you want to come in? Such a different story from last time you were here." His voice is nasty, unforgiving. "Don't you remember leaving us with such unfinished business...for months at that? What is it now? February?" Ry says with disgust.

"But you were keeping things from me, Ry. And you were so *angry*. Now I know things. Things about us. About how I feel about us." I say, trying to encourage him to let me in, but he doesn't.

"Well, I know things, too. And believe it or not, I have a heart, and at this point in our many lives together, it doesn't feel much anymore. Not for you anyway." He laughs, mocking me.

"You know, it used to be that I would pop up in any town you were in, just by sheer want. Sometimes it took multiple lives of yours to find you, but I always *wanted* to. This last time, not so much. My heart is bitter. Made bitter by you, Jade. I want nothing to do with you." His words cut.

I stare at him in disbelief. I blink hard, straining to see him clearly through tears I won't let fall. Tears that are betraying how I feel. His words don't feel true to me, so why is he saying this? He is trying to fill a void. That is all. He doesn't mean these things.

"I wish you were never promised to me, Jade. You make me sick just looking at you here—falling apart at the doorstep of someone you are just now even actually seeing. Well, here I am, Jade... Do you fucking like what you see?" He scoffs then adds,

"Chasing after a Being who has chewed you up and spit you out so many times just for his own fulfillment. That's the problem with mortals and gods, Jade. They do not fucking fit. Not now. Not ever."

If love is supposed to hurt, then this interaction is doing the job with pinpoint precision. I cannot speak. His words burning into my soul. Marking it.

Why is it that some men hold so much anger? Is it because they have to swallow up their feelings like Ry is doing now? Turn inward their emotions so deeply that they can even fool themselves. So hidden and barred by anger that any tears they should shed turn to a river of metallic rage pumping through their blood instead?

He doesn't mean this. I know it's a lie. So why does it still pierce so deep? A lie I can feel because he is of me and I of him. But nonetheless, I feel his next word wholly.

"Pathetic," he whispers down at me. His final word guts me. And then the door slams, like a claim to my worth.

33
THE UNROOTING
RACINE 1979

I wake with the room as empty as my soul. Where spots of light come in with the morning sun, my heart only holds darkness. If putting the ring on opened my eyes to things I felt I had always known, then Ry shutting me out in that moment earlier today ripped my entire world apart.

I am starting to see what has always had to happen. He can't stay, but neither can I. Not mentally at least. For I only know madness now. It was forged in my bones long ago. Something I held onto as the world fell around me, over and over again.

Each life we have together teaching me something new about love. Not the kind I dreamt of as a girl, but the messy, evolving kind that changes who you are—sometimes for better, sometimes not.

One love can awaken a part of you. A part you didn't know existed. Growing into the good of the experience. That's not the one I know.

Then there is another love. A love full of naïve comfort that eats away at your insides. That never leaves, but can't quite stay either, because in all its comfort, you find it is entirely uncomfortable. Ry's love is the latter, and I am completely uncomfortable in all that we are.

And because of it, the same thing would always follow. I would leave tragically, or he would push me away time after time, much like he is doing now. But when the insanity crept in this time, I knew it would stay. Wrap around the crevices of my soul, filling me with fleeting escapes that only I could fathom.

Madness stayed. Madness cradled me. Madness was my undoing, even when he came back in the next life, and became my unrooting, yet again.

I know this now, and after Ry's clear disgust this morning. I knew I could never be the same. I could either break or I could adapt.

Suddenly, all his terrible traits become so clear in my mind. Because sometimes the bad guy will be just that. He may care, show glimpses of someone who could be more. He may even want to be better. But in the end, he's still the villain through and through. And if you are lucky, he'll let you play the villain, too—but it may not be in the way he was hoping.

I am broken, that is true, but free. Free to make a choice that will fucking tear him apart. He was right when he said that mortals and gods do not fit, but I am no fucking mortal, and he is not the god he thinks he is. Our hearts spoke clearly that morning, and what started as two hearts saying I will bleed for you turned, quite tragically, to one saying I will make yours bleed, and that is exactly what I intend to do.

I tear his ring off and stuff it into my bra, my skin already itching from its absence. I no longer wish to wear something so tainted with dishonesty and hatred. Something forged for me in what I mistook for love, only to drain me of my power.

I leave plenty of food for Carya and open the basement door, knowing very well she can travel between realms with no problem, as she did when she disappeared before. The basement door that would send chills to my core, calling me down to its depths. But the basement isn't meant for me tonight.

Ry shattered my heart. He left it in pieces on the floor as if it were a fallen dime-store vase on the mantel. Not even an heirloom worthy enough to be glued back together. No, he made it clear our love was nothing when he spoke that word to me. Pathetic? I will show him how something he sees as so insubstantial can be used to tear his whole world apart.

I slam the front door behind me, so much so that the ancient mirror beside it fractures, my bare feet making hard contact with the wet misty ground once I make my way down the steps. I run toward the trees. The bottoms of my soles already feeling the effects of walking amongst the cold, muddy soil of the southern bayou.

Caked in mud, I run past the sleeping hawk that always lingers around wherever I seem to be. The hawk doesn't sleep tonight, feeling my fevered heart make a direct route to where I know I need to be.

Sweat and tears tangle my hair in a mess against my neck. It isn't even warm here this evening, but the temperature inside me is making me feel as if I am heading to the inferno. A growing fire of fury sitting deep beneath my ribs. I'm afraid not even revenge could smother its flames, but that is the route I must take.

Now the crow's eyes are looking, but I no longer hide as I pass by open moonflowers along the trail. My steps strong and panicked— laughing as I do. My manic state getting the best of me.

I was going to make an example. I would break him from the inside out, much like the soles of my feet upon finding my destination at last. I crawl frantically up to the tree base, ripping at the roots and the soil with hands that will never again show any mercy. Mercy is for the weak. For the breakable. And he will be broken.

I can feel stubborn roots ripping at my cuticles as my female rage seeps into my hands and lets them take on a life of their own. One of my nails bends back, breaking off at its base. Something that should cause me to scream in pain, but no pain compares to what I feel surging through my blackened heart.

Feverishly, I make my way deeper and deeper until I see a light.

Iridescent and welcoming. How deep I am, I do not know, but I pull myself into the mass of entangled roots with only a feeling of how this may turn out.

I am weeping now. An uncontrollable sobbing brought on by the splitting of my unrequited devotion. Weeping for the love I imagined, and so overwhelmingly exhausted by the truth that it will never be.

I am holding onto one moment of vulnerability as two hands grab my arms and pull me farther and farther, until I am in a place I cannot even put words to. But the hands are still there, and they wrap around my shoulders, consoling me in a way they wish someone would reciprocate.

I collapse, finding myself lifted to be cradled and carried away. My tear-soaked vision looking up into the eyes that are receiving me just as I knew they would. The acorn-hued irises rimmed with the ring of the moon. Que.

"Hello, gem. Finally making your own choices, I see."

ACKNOWLEDGMENTS

The magic made within The Rooted Realm Estate owes many thanks to the people who helped make it rooted in reality.

Thank you to Tee for showing me how to adjust my poetic ramblings into something more intentional. Your notes truly helped me take this manuscript to the next level.

Thank you to both Tami and John for gifting me a computer a few holidays ago to make writing this book even possible.

Thank you to Mckenna O'Brien, my lovely sister-in-law, for providing the most beautiful art for the cover. Your art makes this book complete in so many ways.

Thank you so much to my friends, including the ladies of my book club and my neighbors, for being not only my biggest cheerleaders but also amazing beta readers.

Thank you to my dad. My day-one fan. For always encouraging me to write the words within my head, even if it meant we had to miss some of our morning breakfast dates. My poetic ramblings started with you.

Thank you to my mom. My very special first draft reader and the one who made my love for all things spooky bloom. Your excitement about this project kept me excited, even in the moments I thought it was garbage. I took your advice throughout the book to heart, even in the X-rated parts that I boldly cautioned you about in bright pink marker. And your lovely hickory leaves add the sweetest touch to the book.

And to my bro-ha for always hyping me up when I needed it

most. Whether for my book, my dreams, or just plain life in general, your words always hit in the best way.

Thank you to my husband for giving me space and time to see the workings of my mind make it to paper, even if it meant you had to work extra hard to support us, as you always do.

Thank you to my daughter for *always* encouraging me to write, while she created concoctions and took care of her animals. Your love of writing in school gave me an extra incentive. Keep it up!

And thank you to my son for his enthusiasm to read it (although he will get a slightly different version...). And for using it as inspiration for your own school writing projects. That alone made this all worth it.

And to anyone who loves this story. Thank you. It may be garbage to some, but I will keep it in a very special trash can in my heart. I've learned so much on this journey of writing my first novel. I can't wait to put those lessons to use in the sequel, *A Forever Unearthing of Opal and Oak.*

ABOUT THE AUTHOR

Mikki Roule lives in Michigan with her family, where she
uses the woods and the lake as muses for her stories.
She lives with her dashing husband, two fun-loving children, their
lively Shih Tzu puppy, and two cute guinea pigs.